MIKHAIL

A TALE OF PELYTHIA

J. A. KNIGHT

For Magella,
forever perfect

CONTENTS

PROLOGUE

Mikhail was sitting straight, his shoulders rolled back as his mother had taught him. The proper posture of a future king, she had said. He always remembered her advice, and followed it always, even when he was alone. There was nothing more important to him than making his mother proud.

They were leaving the docks. A ceremonial blessing of a ship for the navy's armada had taken them from the castle that morning. The fresh ocean air had made him feel invigorated, the prince wanting to dive into the waves and let them carry him away.

His brother, Yordan, had been bored through the ceremony. Their mother had spent most of her time trying to keep the young boy entertained. She had been spoken to by the king when they had gotten into the carriage. Their father warned her that she had been mothering the boy too much and he had to learn of his responsibilities.

He had watched the younger boy, seeking any kind of recognition on his brother's face for the trouble he had gotten his mother into. But there was no expression on Yordan's face. Nothing except boredom as he stared out the window, watching the streets pass them.

Their mother was tucked against their father's side, his arm protectively draped around her shoulders. She was so pale these days, rarely wearing her heavy crown during their public appearances. It sat in her lap at the moment, her fingers running over the jewels set into the face of it. The king's lips pressed against her forehead in a soft kiss.

"Yordan. Mikhail." She murmured, drawing their attention. "I am proud of you. I know I have said this many times before, but we must be strong and protect each other, or everything we know could be taken from us. You both know this, yes?"

"Of course, Mother." Mikhail answered quickly, his chin lifted slightly in pride.

"Yes, Mama." Yordan mumbled, not really turning his face from the window.

Mikhail elbowed his brother. Where he expected his brother to straighten and give their mother his full attention, the younger boy nudged him back, harder, driving his elbow into his ribs roughly. Mikhail yelped, the sound making their mother jump. It stirred the king, his face turning to them wearing a mask of rage.

"I am sorry, Father." Mikhail said quickly, leaning forward in his seat in an awkward bow.

Yordan copied him, hands held tight in his lap, knuckles white with fear. Mikhail's quick words had soothed the anger they had roused and the king turned back to their mother, pressing his lips to her forehead again. Mikhail could see the minute movements of his father's lips, realising that the man was whispering to her.

He and Yordan straightened from their bows together, sitting in their seats as they had been taught. Mikhail's back was beginning to hurt, but he darned not relax his posture. Yordan slumped beside him, leaning back against the window. He watched his brother, anger simmering beneath his blank expression.

Something caught Yordan's attention further up the street, his head lifting from the hand that supported it. Mikhail leaned slightly, trying to find what Yordan was interested in. A girl was being dragged across the street by her mother ahead of the small envoy. The girl was leaning, craning her neck to watch the carriages move closer. A dark shawl was sliding out of the basket hooked on her arm, unnoticed as it dropped to the ground and was left behind.

Yordan's head whipped around and crystal blue eyes locked on his. Mikhail knew that if he did not step in, Yordan would get himself in trouble. The younger boy's hand started to reach for the handle to the door. The shawl was nearly even with them now, still laying on the ground. He could see the little girl who had dropped it, still leaning back to watch them.

He reached out, pushed his brother back against the seat and burst out of the carriage door. There were yells from behind him, and in the edges of his awareness, he could see the guards around them start in his direction.

Without stopping, Mikhail scooped the shawl from

the ground and strode after the girl. Her mother had stopped dragging her, turning to see what had caused the commotion she could hear behind her. Finally, the girl noticed her shawl was missing, panic springing into her eyes.

Mikhail held out the shawl, breaking into a short jog to cover the last distance between them. He could hear the guards behind him, but they stopped as he did. The shawl was held between them, the girl staring at him in fear.

"Neassa, thank him for returning your... shawl." The mother murmured.

Deep brown eyes stared at him, the girl unwilling to close the distance. She shuffled in place before snatching out a hand to take back her shawl. It was only once it had left his hands that Mikhail realised how silky and smooth it had felt against his skin. An expensive shawl to lose, for a commoner.

"Neassa."

"Thank you." Neassa mumbled, her head dropping now so she didn't have to look at him.

"My prince. We must return to the carriages." A guard murmured behind him.

"Of course." Mikhail gave a slight bow of his head then turned on his heel and allowed the guards to guide him back to safety.

He could already hear his mother's crying, and he knew the expression that the king would have. Mikhail should have let Yordan take the punishment he wanted. Squaring his shoulders, Mikhail climbed the step back into the carriage, masking his expression to take his punishment like a man.

CHAPTER ONE

Mikhail strode down the hall, his posture befitting a prince. The king had summoned him and he would comply shortly. As soon as he'd finished talking to his brother. It would be better that he be late for the king's summons than Yordan be punished for staying in bed longer than the king approved of. The morning was nearly done and he had yet to see his little brother.

Yordan's door was still closed and Mikhail knocked. He did not wait for a response, merely opening the door and stepping through. As he had suspected, Yordan was still in bed, the blankets pulled over his head. Mikhail sighed. He may be later to the king's side than he had thought.

"Wake up, brother." Mikhail said, closing a hand around his brother's ankle and shaking him.

The reaction was immediate, Yordan jerking his foot out of the hold, sitting up, a dagger in his hand. The sunlight glinted off the sharp edge. His brother's eyes were wide and fearful, darting to the shadows of the room then back to Mikhail.

"Why must you wake me like that, Mikhail?" Yordan rasped. "I could have hurt you."

"I do not think so, Yordan." Mikhail shook his head, dropping himself down on the end of Yordan's bed. "You have become slow. Your mourning is getting out of hand."

"Do not tell me that it is out of hand." Yordan hissed. "You would not even talk to anyone for a month after Mother passed."

"Do not talk to me of Mother."

"I will. You will not lecture me." Yordan spat.

Mikhail stood, running a hand through his hair. "This girl... You knew her for less than a week. You have always been soft, Yordan, but this is taking it too far. You need to strengthen your heart. Father will not tolerate weakness."

"Emotions are not weakness." Yordan sighed, the tension and anger leaving his body.

"They are not. But Father thinks they are. Do not anger him."

"I do not care what Father thinks."

"You should." Mikhail spoke softly. "You are to be married soon, to a foreign princess. Do you think Father will tolerate you staying in bed all hours of the day once she has arrived?"

"I do not see why I should be the one to marry her." Yordan muttered.

A mask settled over Mikhail's expression, leaving nothing for Yordan to read. "It is what he decided. Be glad, brother, I have decided to take your place in the throne room today. Pull yourself out of your despair, before you humiliate us all."

A pillow hit the back of his head. Mikhail paused in the doorway then closed the door behind him. He sighed deeply, his fingers brushing against a scar on his forearm. A scar he had gotten from defending Yordan from their father's wrath. It was not the only mark that marred his body, but it was the only one he had received from his father.

His footsteps echoed in the hall as he walked away, hoping that his brother would get out of bed. The foreign princess was to arrive that day. Mikhail had no idea what to expect. She was from a culture of matriarchy, where theirs was ruled by men. Would she expect them to bow to her will, or would she be educated enough not to step outside the confines of a woman's place in their culture?

"Your Highness." A servant woman bowed in front of him, breaking him from his thoughts.

"Yes?"

"His Majesty is asking who will be joining him." She mumbled.

Mikhail clicked his tongue in irritation, he was not late yet. Yordan had agitated him so quickly that he had left without having a full conversation with his brother. And yet even so, the king was already asking for his presence.

He dismissed the servant girl with a wave of his hand and strode on. "I am heading there now."

The peasants that lined the hall to the throne room shuffled out of his way, none daring to meet his eye as he passed them. He nodded to the guard that opened the door for him and Mikhail stepped into the silence of the throne room. Lifting his eyes from the floor, he met his father's gaze. A chill ran down his spine and, without the king speaking, Mikhail took up his place beside the king. Standing with his hands clasped behind his back, he settled in the most comfortable position he could manage.

"You are late." The king murmured.

"No. The sword has not been brought to you. You have not spoken the ritual words. You are merely trying to guilt me."

There was a soft sound from the man in front of him, but nothing more was said. Two servant men shuffled into the room, carrying an ornate box between them. They knelt, holding the box up to the king. He opened the lid, revealing the decorative sword that nestled into velvet inside the box.

Gemstones sparkled in the hilt, laid into gold. It was not a sword of death, but of beauty and truth.

Diamonds, emeralds and sapphires filled much of the hilt. Amethysts, moonstones and topaz filled the empty spaces between.

Mikhail wanted to take up the sword himself, but kept his hands clasped tightly behind him as the king lifted it easily from its resting place. The blade was laid across his lap, one hand resting on the flat of it, the other still curled around the hilt. The king's head was bowed and he murmured too softly for anyone to hear.

He could hear the words in his head, whispered in his mother's voice. "I call upon the magic, to divine true from false. I call upon the light, to banish the darkness. I call upon the sword, to cut through the veil and unmask deceptions. Guide me to the truth."

"We can begin." The king announced, lifting his head from his prayer over the blade.

An old man came through the door, his weight held

up by a shaky walking stick. Mikhail's mind started to wander, half-listening to the man as he began a plea to the king. Something about his neighbour's animals being let into his land and eating the food he needed for his own beasts.

The voices droned on and on, Mikhail's mind wandering further. His father was allowing his brother to marry a foreign princess. A princess from a culture that was ruled by their women. He understood why the king would not allow him to marry her. While Mikhail was on the throne, her and her children would never have the chance to take their kingdom from them.

"You were not listening to anything that was said." The king murmured, breaking into his thoughts. Mikhail shook himself slightly. "You gave the man some coin to buy the food he needed and ordered some of the guards to accompany him home so that they might talk to his neighbour who is overstepping his bounds. I also know that you are going to order an investigation into why the neighbour is purposely stealing from the old man and assist him if you can."

There was no response from his father, Mikhail knowing he had irritated the man. The king always wished to be right. Mikhail not listening would have made him very happy. It would have been something else to lord over him, to belittle him for. Something he would never have done had Mikhail's mother still lived. He had become bitter and cruel since her death.

Their morning passed slowly, complaint after complaint being laid at their feet. Mikhail offered advice when he was asked, his father correcting any mistakes he made. So many people asked for protection from their own actions. From debts and failed business ventures, to lost goods and stolen wares. It weighed heavily on Mikhail.

This time a woman entered the room, her dark hair glossy and hanging in tight ringlets down her back. Deep brown eyes lifted higher than most commoners dared and stared hard at his face. Mikhail frowned down at her. A long moment later she finally bowed her head, eyes dropping to the floor. A simple shift covered her form, and in her hand was a woven basket with a neatly folded shawl inside.

The shawl seemed familiar, but Mikhail could not think of where he knew it from. There was no reason he would recognise anything about this woman. She was tanned a dark brown, a commoner, probably a farm girl.

Mikhail, contrary to the servant's beliefs, did not go hunting for farming girls to bed. He had no desire to spread bastard children throughout the city. It would have hurt his mother if she still lived. His father would have disapproved. Disapproved and spirited away the girl to avoid scandal.

"My king." Her voice rang out, bowing low to Mikhail's father. "I stand here, before the sword of true divining and speak words that are no lie."

Her words stirred him, and Mikhail looked to the king to see his reaction. The king had lent forward in his seat, his grip on the sword's hilt turning his knuckles white. There was a silence that stretched between them.

"An old vow." The king finally answered. "Speak, child."

"By the ancient laws of our world, I lay claim to what is mine."

"What is it that you claim, child?" The king asked, the grip on the sword not relaxing.

Mikhail was confused. This woman was acting as though the king would grant her any wish. She spoke with such a honeyed voice, her words leaving her lips with a more songlike rhythm than a normal conversation. Her gaze kept flicking to him, their eyes meeting frequently.

"I claim the hand of the Crown Prince Mikhail, of House Nemes, to be my husband." Her chin lifted, meeting the king's eyes squarely.

"No."

"By traditions that have been bound with magic, he is mine." She continued, ignoring the king's refusal. "Nothing short of death will free us from the bond."

"Then you will die." The king stood, brandishing the sword at the woman.

Mikhail did not know what to do. His father was trembling, staring down at the commoner with such fierce hatred. The woman did not seem to care, her chin lifted high. She was no longer looking at Mikhail, her focus on the aging king before her. He sighed, stepping between his father and the woman.

"Enough." Mikhail said, putting his hand on his father's shoulder. "You will not have her killed, Father. What is she talking about?"

The king sat slowly, waving his hand. "Leave us. All of you. I will see no more."

The servants bowed, trickling out of the throne room. There was a brief cry from outside the main doors as the waiting crowd was turned away. Soon silence settled over them. Mikhail stepped back, looking between his father and the woman. How had she caused so much anger in his father with nothing but a few incredulous words.

"I will not give my son to one of your kind." The king hissed.

"Then you would see a foreign princess take the throne instead?" She asked.

"Who are you?" Mikhail snapped, sick of them speaking about him as if he were not there.

Dark eyes turned to him again. "My name is Neassa. It is good to see you again, Mikhail."

"Again?"

"Mikhail, that is enough." The king growled. "You will not take my son, and neither will I allow you to sit on the throne."

"Then you lose your country." Neassa shrugged. "I at least see you as my king. I want this less than you. But the bond cannot be broken."

"Death will free him." The king murmured.

Neassa shook her head. "I will not allow you to kill me. Nor will my people forgive you if you cause my death in any way."

"Will someone explain to me what is going on?" Mikhail shouted. "You talk as though you are taking her seriously, Father. She looks like nothing more than a farming girl. Why does she have a claim on me?"

"Does he know nothing about his own kingdom?" Neassa asked. "About his subjects?"

"Do not say it as if I am a fool." Mikhail growled.

"He knows what he needs to for now." The king snarled.

She laughed. "Mikhail, your father has been hiding things from you. The sword was made by one of my people. A thousand years ago. It is blessed and imbued with magic. It gives you the power to know if a person is lying. That is why he is reacting the way he is. I have not spoken a lie since I recited the vow."

"Father?" Mikhail turned to the old king, searching his face.

A vein in the king's forehead throbbed. Mikhail waited, the king would not stay silent forever. Not with the threat of Neassa answering for him.

"She speaks the truth." The king admitted. "Her people have a long history with our kingdom."

Mikhail combed his fingers through his hair. "What people? Why am I bound to her?"

"I can show you." Neassa broke in. "Then you can decide what you wish to do."

"No-"

"Yes!" She snapped at the king. "Let your son choose his own life."

"How can I trust that you will not enchant him?" The king asked.

Neassa laughed again, the sound making Mikhail's heart thump. "That is not my people's power, my king. You have nothing to fear. I will not steal away your precious son if he wishes to return."

"I will go with you." Mikhail answered.

There was a deep sigh from his father, but Mikhail found he did not care. He could not be treated like a child but be expected to shoulder the responsibility of a man. His father would have to treat him as an equal. He was going to be given the crown in a few years, there should be no secrets about his own kingdom.

"You will have to change your clothes." Neassa smiled. "The harbour does not see many rich folk unless they are sailing. Do you have anything less regal?"

"My son-"

"Will make his own choices." Neassa interrupted again. "No harm will come to him while I am at his side."

Mikhail glanced down at the sword. That was the second time that Neassa had interrupted his father, and yet the king had not struck her down. He turned, moving down the dias steps to stop at her side. She was beautiful, Mikhail realised. Beautiful and brave.

"Mikhail." The king murmured. "Be wary."

"I will, Father." Mikhail bowed slightly.

Neassa turned, striding from the throne room. Mikhail followed after her, watching the way her hair bounced with each step. His eyes moved down, following the sway of her hips. She stopped, turning to face him. Quickly, Mikhail's eyes lifted back up to her face. There was a smile on her lips and Mikhail realised she knew where he had been looking.

"I have never been in a castle before." She admitted. "Where is your room? I will help you find something to wear so you blend in."

"Why are we going to the harbour?" Mikhail asked.

"Do you know of anywhere else with a large body of water? The lake is too far." Neassa tilted her head.

"I... know of a place." He said softly. "But I do not think I should take you there."

She laughed. "Because of your father? You have defied him already today, what is another going to do?"

Mikhail studied the woman, her expression slowly turning from jubilant to curious as she studied him in return. There was a tiny scar on her left cheek, like something had punctured the skin. A strand of hair fell across her face and she brushed it back quickly. He took her hand gently. Her nails were cut short, but her palms were soft, uncalloused and smooth.

"Who are you exactly?" Mikhail asked, releasing her.

Neassa smiled broadly. "Take me to the water and I'll show you."

CHAPTER TWO

"Are you taking me somewhere quiet to kill me?"
Neassa asked with a laugh.

She was looking at the rough stone walls that formed
the passageway they were walking through. Mikhail
paused as Neassa ran her hand over the wall. When
she noticed him looking, her bright smile returned,
her hand dropping to her side.

"Do you always stare at girls like that?"

"I was not staring." Mikhail turned away from her.
"Let us continue."

Her bare feet made very little noise as she followed
him. Mikhail had to glance back every few seconds to
assure himself that she was still there. Each time he
turned she gave him a bright smile, the basket
swinging back and forth in her hands. He was not
sure what to make of her.

The passage ended, opening up into a large cavern.
Mikhail set down the lantern he had been using to

light their way. Neassa was calm, looking around the darkness with interest. She moved forward without hesitation, stepping calmly over a small ledge that Mikhail knew was there but could not see.

"These pools, what are they?" She asked.

Mikhail looked into the inky darkness below, the pools hidden by the deep shadows of the cavern. How had she known they were there? Only the royal family was allowed in this place. So sacred that even the servants were forbidden entrance and any that were found inside were disposed of.

"How do you know the pools are there?" He asked softly.

"I can see in the dark." Neassa answered.

She was hidden by the darkness now. Mikhail could hear her bare feet moving along the damp ground. There was a rustling of material and Mikhail, unable to restrain his curiosity, took up the lantern and followed Neassa into the cavern. Neassa was standing by one of the pools, her dress pooled around her feet.

"What are-" Mikhail started.

"I have my shawl." Neassa smiled back at him. "You will not see anything. Come closer. It will be easier to show you."

Mikhail kicked off his boots and continued down to her side. He glanced down at the pool she was standing next to. Not this one. She stepped forward before he could speak. His hand gripped her arm, pulling her back from it.

"What are you doing?" Neassa gasped, fear showing for the first time.

He released her quickly, ashamed at how tight he had grabbed her. "Not that one. There is another further in."

She settled at his words, a hand laying over the place he'd grabbed. Her frame was hidden within the folds of her shawl, wrapped loosely around her. His eyes wandered down, following the length of her legs. There was a soft laugh and Mikhail pulled his eyes back to her face.

"My apologies." Mikhail murmured and moved forward to guide her.

The shadows swayed with the lantern light. It didn't reach to the edges of the room, but the smooth floor under Mikhail's feet guided him confidently towards the larger pool. Neassa let out a soft gasp beside him and hurried forward.

"It's beautiful!" Neassa's voice echoed through the cavern. "Can I touch this one?"

"Yes."

Mikhail stepped forward, the lantern spilling light over Neassa's tanned face. She was smiling up at him, crouched beside the pool. It was larger than the circle of light the lantern provided and unlike the other, it had no bottom that he and his brother had ever found. He crouched down beside Neassa, careful not to look in her direction.

"This is ocean water." Neassa murmured, leaning forward and dipping her fingers into the water. "It must seep up through tunnels in the cliffs. That is amazing. Does the water ever leave?"

"Not that I have seen." Mikhail answered softly. "I do not often visit the cavern."

He saw Neassa tilt her head at him. She moved, Mikhail's eyes drawn to her legs as she stepped down into the pool. The water rippled out from her. Surprisingly, her shawl didn't float across the surface of the water, it clung to her, keeping her form hidden. Mikhail glanced away, ashamed again that he couldn't stop looking at her.

"Mikhail. You need to watch now." Neassa murmured. "Do not look away."

"You are not clothed." Mikhail replied, keeping his eyes averted.

"I will be wearing a different skin."

The words made him turn, Neassa's face close to his. Her eyes were inky black, only the thinnest ring of colour around the edges. She pushed back from the edge, dipping her head under the water and slicking her hair back from her face. Her shawl was clinging to her, restricting her from kicking her legs.

"Neassa." Mikhail started, reaching out a hand to her as she started to sink.

Her face warped, eyes growing larger and shifting to the side of her face. The shawl melded to her skin, her legs fusing together. Mikhail stumbled back from the water in horror, unable to look away as Neassa transformed. She spun in the water and hefted her body up onto the ledge beside him.

A seal was sitting on the stone, Neassa's body gone and replaced with the animal's. Mikhail shuffled backwards, dragging the lantern with him. What had happened? What had he just witnessed? The animal looked at him then dragged itself back into the water. Slowly, Mikhail approached the edge of the pool. Neassa's face broke the surface, her lips curved into a bright smile. She stepped out of the pool, water rushing from her shawl and down her legs. The material still clung to her body, hiding much less than it had before.

"What are you?" He asked.

"A selkie." Neassa answered, sitting next to him. Mikhail watched her wring out her hair, water splashing over him. The curls dried quickly, bouncing as she moved her head. There was a sly smile on her face as she glanced at him, slender fingers tugging her shawl tighter around her body. He looked away, unsure what questions he should be asking of the woman.

"Has your father really not told you of us?" Neassa asked, shuffling closer.

"No."

"We live in the harbour. Most of the seals you see are my people." Neassa explained, trailing her fingers through the water again. "We have a city of sorts in the cliffs. The rock has been tunnelled through for centuries."

"Could this connect to one of your tunnels?" Mikhail asked, gesturing to the pool.

"Perhaps. But there are many cracks and crevasses in the rocks as well. There are many places the water could have come from. Why do you ask?"

"My mother..." Mikhail trailed off.

"She was sick." Neassa murmured. "It was a time of great mourning when she died."

Mikhail nodded. "She would come to these pools and soak in them for hours at a time. She said that she always felt stronger after being here. But if it is just normal sea water... then she was lying."

Laughter surprised him, Nessa's head thrown back as the merry sound left her. She settled after a long moment, glancing at him with her dark eyes. He met her gaze, his jaw clenched in anger.

"Do not scowl like that Mikhail." Neassa smiled. "Your mother was not lying. The sea is more than just water. It holds a magic that we cannot use. It is far more powerful than you can imagine."

"Is that how you can change your form?" Mikhail asked. "How is it that we are bound?"

Neassa ran her fingers down the shawl. "It is in my blood. This shawl is my seal skin. It has no straight edges like a woven shawl. There is magic in it. Just as there is in the ocean. It is our curse that if someone takes our skin, we must stay with them, to be their wife and raise their children."

"But I have never met you before."

"You have. But we were children. I dropped my shawl. You chased after me to return it even though the guards were at your heels." Neassa smiled. "If you had kept the shawl, I would have stayed by your side, forever searching for my skin so I could return to my home beneath the waves."

"I returned it, so are you not free?" Mikhail asked.

"No. Less so." Neassa sighed, resting her chin on her knees and staring off into the darkness. "Your kindness invoked a bond that not even my mother knew of. A longing to share my life with you. Because you gave me the freedom to choose, even if you were not aware of it at the time."

"That makes no sense." Mikhail said. "How does me giving you your freedom mean that you want to stay by my side?"

She laughed again, brushing hair back from her face. "I asked my mother the same question. It has been many generations since we have lost someone to a skin-thief. We have not been stolen from the sea. We have not longed for our true home."

"And you would give it up to spend your life with me?" Mikhail questioned.

Neassa shook her head. "I will never give up the sea. But magic is not easily reversed."

Mikhail stood, carrying the lantern with him. Neassa looked up at him, an easy smile on her face. He could not deny that she looked beautiful, sitting there in nothing but a shawl, her hair hanging loose about her face. So different from the painted noble women.

"What happens if I deny you?"

Pain flashed across Neassa's face. Her head turned away, and Mikhail's heart squeezed tightly at the thought that he had hurt this woman. He had only met her a short hour ago and already he never wanted to hurt her.

"I return to my people and we never see each other again." Neassa said softly. "But the bond will remain. You have felt it before now, as a deep longing in your heart."

"We know nothing of each other." Mikhail sighed.

"Has that ever stopped anyone before?" She asked.

He looked away into the darkness, thinking of his mother. There had been nothing his father could do to save his wife. Mikhail had watched his father's pain and decided that he never wanted to feel that heartbreak for himself. Morning for love would never happen for him, that is what he had always told himself.

His duty was to marry one of the daughters of a noble family and renegotiate the peace that had grown tenuous among the ruling class when his father, and grandfather, decided to marry women from the common folk. Mikhail looked at Neassa. No matter if she was or was not a selkie, she was a commoner. The nobles would never accept her.

"What are you thinking about?" She asked.

Mikhail did not meet her gaze as he answered. "I cannot take you as my wife. I will not take you as my wife. We will end up despising each other. Come and get dressed. I will escort you to the gates."

Her shoulders began to shake, though Mikhail could not hear any sounds of crying. His heart pained. He knew he had hurt her so deeply, but he would not take her. He would not expose her to danger.

Reaching down, Mikhail took her arm and pulled her to her feet. She stumbled, leaning heavily on him until she regained her balance. Her arm was pulled from his hold and she tugged her shawl tighter around her shoulders. Neassa would not look at him. It was only the briefest warmth against his side, but he longed for it to return. He controlled himself, unwilling to give her false hope for a moment of comfort. Mikhail began leading the way back to the entrance, the lantern held tight in his hand. The darkness pressed harder on him, whispering to him to stumble and fall.

Her dress was where she had left it, a mess of fabric on the ground. Neassa stumbled forward, picking it up and pulling it over her body. Mikhail looked away, waiting for her to finish dressing. There was still silence from the woman, though Mikhail could hear her heavy breathing as she tried to control herself. His eyes were drawn down to the pool beside him. The pool his mother had soaked in for most of his memories of her. He could see her there now, smiling up at him, a simple white shift protecting her modesty. She had the same simple beauty as Neassa, with no need for the paints and trinkets the other noble women used.

"I am ready to leave." Neassa whispered.

It was like all life had been drained from her, the joy that had made her voice bright was gone. Mikhail turned, catching sight of her face before she looked away. Tears streaked down her cheeks, gathering at her chin.

"Let us go." Mikhail replied, gesturing to the door. Neassa walked slowly, mounting the steps that would lead them out. There was no echoing laughter as there had been when they entered. It was only the sound of their footsteps now. They moved out into the rough stone passage and started back, not a single word passing between them.

Mikhail watched Neassa walk, the sway of her hips subdued, her head bowed as she hid her emotions. He stepped forward as they reached the end of the passageway and opened the door for her. She glanced at him through her hair, Mikhail meeting her gaze without hesitation.

Neassa stepped out into the hall, grasping her basket to her chest. Before Mikhail could stop her, she was running. He watched her turn the corner and out of sight. A servant girl peered around the same corner, dropping into a quick bow when she realised who she was looking at. Mikhail sighed, closing the door behind him.

It was better this way, he told himself. The life of a royal was not for those weak of heart. Like his mother. This was not the life for a commoner. Not even one like Neassa. She would not thrive. He was doing this for her own good. Maybe she would realise that one day.

He walked slowly back to his rooms, ignoring the servants that moved around him. The last expression he had seen on Neassa's face was one of deep pain. It was fitting. Mikhail had hurt her so deeply, that he should never be forgiven, not even by himself. She was saved from a life fraught with dangers. Saved from a life that would never truly welcome her.

CHAPTER THREE

The formal robes were uncomfortable on Mikhail's frame. He was looking down on his brother, watching the younger man walk his bride to the altar. Yordan looked pained. The woman beside him was unhappy, judging from the downward curve of her mouth. They were both pawns in their family's eyes. She had been sent here by her sister. Mikhail pitied them both.

A young woman sat at his side, a daughter of one of the noble houses, he could not remember which one. She had her face hidden behind a layer of paints, a fan held before her. Mikhail disliked her, and the way she would touch his arm. It was like an old grandmother, weak but grasping fingers tugging at his clothes. This was the one that his father told him would solve many of the problems they faced.

Yordan reached the altar and the pair knelt, heads bowed before the king. They recited vows, their voices soaring high over the crowd that gathered to watch. Mikhail knew that his time would come soon to kneel at that altar and be bound to a woman. He hoped the one beside him would catch sick and die. Anything to be free of her grasping fingers.

The king drew out a rope woven from silk. He drew their hands together and wrapped the silk around them, physically binding them. They would remain that way for a week. There could be no secrets between man and wife, not even those of bodily functions. The commoners only remained bound like that until the night was through. Mikhail thought them lucky.

Yordan and his bride stood, carefully turning to face the crowd. Cheers threatened to bring down the roof. White flower petals were thrown over the couple, and blessings were shouted from many lips. Mikhail stepped forward, stopping his brother before they could leave and present themselves to the commoners that crowded outside the castle walls.

"I wish you great happiness, brother." He said softly.

"I hope that it comes to pass." Yordan murmured back.

The silent woman beside him did not look, staring straight ahead. Her face was a mask molded into a slight smile, one that did not reach her eyes. Mikhail stepped in front of her, forcing her to look up at him. For a moment he was struck by how much her face reminded him of Neassa. But anger flared in her eyes and the resemblance ended. Her head dipped into the slightest of bows towards him.

"My lord." She murmured through clenched teeth.

"My lady." Mikhail replied.

They parted, Mikhail had no words to comfort a

woman who despised her new life. Would Neassa have given him the same angry look if he had accepted her? He pushed the thought from his mind. She was gone, and they would never see each other again. That was all he could do for her, to save her from a life she was unprepared for.

"I will be waiting in the hall." Mikhail murmured and stepped back.

Yordan gave him a tight smile as they started the slow walk to the castle gates, hands bound together.

Mikhail watched them leave. Fingers tugged at his sleeve and he turned to acknowledge his companion for the event. Her fan fluttered by her face but she did not speak. The silence irritated him.

"Let us continue ahead." He murmured, offering her his arm.

She took it, though their limbs barely touched. Mikhail led her through the corridors, following the crowd to the hall where Yordan would enjoy his wedding feast. Hundreds of nobles had gathered, and the bride's brothers had travelled with her across the sea to deliver their sister safely.

"Prince Mikhail." A steward bowed. "You will be seated on the dias with your brother."

"Where is the king seated?" Mikhail asked politely.

"The king will not be joining the festivities." The man replied, eyes darting across the floor. "He has taken to his chambers. He claims to be unwell."

Mikhail sighed. "Very well. Have the princess' brothers been seated at the dias also?"

"Yes, Prince Mikhail. As we were told."

"Continue with your tasks." Mikhail dismissed him.

His companion plucked lightly at his sleeve. Mikhail ignored the touch. If she wished to communicate with

him, she would do so with her tongue. He would not
tolerate being tugged at as if she was a small child with
no manners or proper upbringing. They moved
through the hall, the crowd parting for them, and
Mikhail sat on his brother's left hand side. Two men
sat on the right of the table. The princess' brothers,
he assumed.

"What is your brother like?" One of them asked,
leaning over. "Will he treat my sister well?"

Mikhail glanced at the tanned man. "You ask me?
Would I not lie to protect my brother's image?"

Anger formed in the other man's face but Mikhail
lifted his hand to stop it. He had no desire to start an
argument with the princess' family. Not when she was
already so angry about her fate.

"My brother is a good man. He treats all those around
him fairly and equally. She is in good hands and will
come to no harm from him." Mikhail replied. "Now,
drink, be merry. Your sister will be safe in our lands.
We will not let anything happen to her."

His words did not seem to comfort the man, but he
sank back into his seat, playing with the wine jug
before him. Mikhail watched him for some time,
ignoring the tugging on his other sleeve. The two
brothers began to talk quietly, Mikhail unable to hear
their words. It was far more interesting than the
woman at his side. He would have to pass her off to
another man soon. She should at least have some
attention cast her way before the night ended.

The crowd settled slowly into their seats, joyful
chatter filling the air. With the king not in attendance,
the mood was relaxed. Mikhail wondered why his
father had not come. He was always talking of
responsibility and tradition, and yet he had refused to

join this celebration. It was unfair, Mikhail thought. The king should be here to watch over his sons.

"They are coming!" A reveller yelled into the hall. Silence fell quickly and Mikhail rose to his feet. The hall followed his lead quickly, their glasses raised to the door in a silent salute. As the doors opened to admit Yordan and his bride, a cheer went through the crowd. White petals were thrown over them again, clinging to their hair and clothes. The princess brushed them from her face, her face an expression of perfectly polite joy.

Yordan led her to the dias and helped her into her seat, a difficult task with their hands bound together. Mikhail sat with his brother, the revellers following suit. A few mere moments later the hall had erupted into conversation and cheers. The prince and his bride were now forgotten, their tribute had been made, it was time for food and drink.

"Brother, where is Father?" Yordan asked.

"Not here." Mikhail sighed. "He has taken to his chambers. He told the steward he was ill, but it is more likely that he is drinking himself into a stupor. It is not our place to question him."

There was a soft sigh from Yordan. "I had hoped he would join us. Kismet refuses to allow the binding to remain for the full week. I am unsure what to do."

He had thought this would happen. "It is simply a clash between cultures. We will have to talk to her."

"I can hear every word you are saying." The princess hissed, leaning onto Yordan's shoulder to glare at him. "I am not dumb or mute. I will not keep this binding on. It is uncomfortable and his hand is damp."

Mikhail smiled. "I know this is not how things are

done in your country. But it is how it is done here. If you remove the binding before the week, then you will not be married by our laws. You will be a princess without a realm."

"That is what has happened already." She hissed. "You think I wanted to be my sister's pawn?"

"You think I want to be my father's?" Yordan hissed back, pushing her off his shoulder. "I had no wish to marry you, not because of who you are, but because it was not my choice. Do not make this more difficult for us."

"Do not make it more difficult?" Kismet shouted, her voice ringing through the hall and silencing those around them. "I have been forced to come to a land where women are treated little better than cattle. I could have been a queen, I could have ruled without a need to take a husband."

"You are not there any longer." Mikhail stood, his voice rising to match hers. "If you have to direct your anger at someone, direct it at your sister. She is the one who sent you here to this hellish place, as you seem to think it is. She chose you."

The woman's head bowed. She made no response and, slowly, the celebration returned, the men already too drunk to hold the serious atmosphere for long. Women glanced at Kismet throughout the feast, watching her downcast posture. Mikhail caught the eyes of several young women, their gazes shifting from him quickly.

"If you tug on my sleeve again, I will have you escorted back to your father." Mikhail growled. "Speak, woman, if you have a tongue in your mouth." The hand dropped from his sleeve. "I wish to go home." Came the soft, wavering voice.

"Then go." Mikhail grunted, lifting his cup again. There was the rustle of material and Mikhail felt the presence at his side move away. He was free of one annoyance. If only he could rid his brother of the one that was chained to him. His eyes followed the woman as she made her way swiftly from the hall, side stepping a few groping hands. Mikhail noted those that had attempted to touch her, they would be punished come the morn.

He stood, crossing behind Yordan and Kismet to tap one of her brothers on the shoulder. "May I sit here for a moment?"

The brother looked like he was going to curse, but a wave of Kismet's hand sent him from the seat. Mikhail was amused, how easily he was controlled. Slipping in beside her, Mikhail studied her closely for the first time. She shared many similarities with Neassa, but there was a regalness that only came from someone born into their life.

"What is it?" Kismet asked. "Come to chastise me further in front of the people?"

"I would never dream of it." Mikhail smiled. "I have come to offer peace. My words were harsh, that is true, and I should not have spoken of your sister like that. I only said what I did to protect my brother."

"I can hear you." Yordan murmured. "Just as she could hear us."

Mikhail lifted his gaze over Kismet's head. "I am not talking to you brother, entertain yourself with your wine."

There was a grunt from Yordan and the cup lifted to his lips. Mikhail shook his head, he had hoped that his brother's bride would be a gentle soul, someone to help lift the younger man from his sorrows. Instead he got a warrior. But perhaps it would work out in the end.

"You talk to him as if he is a child." Kismet spoke.

"He is, to me." Mikhail replied. "He has always made irresponsible choices, or not thought before he acted. He is a child. I had hoped he would be paired with a gentle lady. But we must make do with what fate has decided."

Kismet quirked an eyebrow. "And what is it that you wish for me to do."

"Train him. You are strong and independent. Yordan is- brother, close your ears lest you get hurt- a sensitive boy. I have done all I can to strengthen his heart, but he does not belong in this life. You understand." Mikhail quirked an eyebrow back at her. "Your sister, I imagine, has had to fight to keep her throne, even from her brothers, or those outside that think a man would be better suited."

"In some ways, yes." Kismet admitted. "But our realm is more stable than this one."

Mikhail nodded. "A blessing, I'm sure. All I ask is that you do not go easy on my brother. If you find weakness in him, remove it however you wish."

Surprise crossed Kismet's face for a moment as she studied him in return. "Why are you making peace?"

"I have no desire to fight those that will be closest to me. We are family now, even if we do not wish it. And family is all we have to protect us." Mikhail echoed his mother's words. "There may be a day where I will need your help on planning for battle. Or protecting my brother. I care not where help comes from, only that it exists. Will you try to tolerate my brother?"

"Only tolerate? You do not wish me to love him?"

"That is for you to decide. I cannot command emotions." Mikhail rose from his seat. "But I do ask for loyalty."

Kismet stared up at him and then turned away, not giving any answer. Mikhail did not expect one and moved from her brother's seat. The man glared at him before he sat and, when he leaned to talk to his sister, Kismet waved him away. Relief spread through Mikhail, that had gone better than he hoped, the princess would consider his proposal. She would be a great ally if she chose to be.

There was nothing more he could do for now, merely hope that his brother did not ruin the tentative agreement between himself and Kismet. He sunk back into his seat, watching the hall devolve from noble celebration to a more base unruliness. Several nobles were now secluded in corners, their mouths glued to each other. Amusement swept through him as he saw that quite a few of those couples were not couples that had walked in together. There would be fights before the night was out, and Mikhail planned to watch each one.

CHAPTER FOUR

Mikhail stirred, his eyes opening on his dark room. He sat up slowly, peering into the dark corners. For a moment he thought of Neassa and how little the darkness had bothered her sight. There it was again, a scuffing sound across the rug. Was there someone in his room?

"Yordan? Go back to your wife. It has been a week, you cannot start hiding from her in here simply because the binding is removed now." Mikhail groaned.

"Die!" A girl's voice screamed and she darted at him. A thin blade was raised in her hand. Mikhail had no chance to respond, his hands too slow to flick aside the blanket they had been trapped under. But the blade never landed. It hovered in the air, catching the moonlight on its edge.

"I told you to leave him." Neassa's voice whispered through the room. "Why would you not listen?"

The blade was dropped harmlessly on the bed and Mikhail snatched it up. The girl was shoved back, toppling to the floor with a soft shriek. Mikhail moved to light a candle, the room too dark to see clearly.

"Are you harmed?" Neassa asked.

"No." Mikhail murmured, fumbling with his tinder box.

"Someone is coming." The girl murmured from the floor.

Something hit him in the dark and Mikhail felt the bed under his back. There was a weight on his waist, holding him down. Then Neassa's lips were on his. They were soft and full. He could taste the ocean on them. She started to pull away but he tangled his fingers into her hair, holding her to him. The doors slammed open, disrupting them.

"My lor-!" A cry was choked off.

A lantern swung in one guard's grip, throwing light around the room wildly. Neassa pulled back, keeping her hair covering her face. Anger started in Mikhail's stomach and he sat up, arms wrapping around Neassa to stop her from falling off his lap. Silently, he turned to study the guards that stood in his doorway, brandishing swords at them. They could see Neassa's nude form in the places his arms could not cover her.

"Forgive us." The older man said, bowing deeply. "We thought we heard a cry for help."

"Leave." Mikhail growled.

The doors closed, leaving them in silence. Mikhail was very aware of Neassa's warmth in his lap and his arms. She smelled of the ocean, all open air and deep water. Drawing her close, Mikhail pressed his lips to hers again. He had never allowed himself a moment of weakness around a woman and Neassa was far softer than he had expected.

"Get off her!" The girl hissed, appearing at their side. Mikhail reluctantly released the selkie, staring at her as she twisted out of his lap and withdrew. Her shawl was wrapped around her shoulders by the young girl that had tried to harm him. His gaze turned to her, studying the new face. She scowled at him, her arms crossed over her chest. He flipped the knife and offered her the handle.

"You are giving it back to me?" She asked, surprised.

"Niamh." Neassa hissed. "Do not take it."

The younger girl, Niamh, scowled at Neassa. "It is mine."

"She may have it Neassa. It matters not." Mikhail pressed the dagger into the girl's hand.

Neassa turned away from him further, her face nearly buried in the curtains that hung in his room. Mikhail stalked forward, his hand touching her shoulder and finding the smooth surface of her shawl. Turning the woman towards him, he was struck by the desire to pull her seal skin away and see her body again.

"Please do not touch me." Neassa murmured. "You have already dismissed me once."

"Touch her and I will put a hole in your side." Niamh hissed from beside him.

Mikhail dropped his hands, stepping back from them both. "I assume you are a selkie also, Niamh?"

She clutched her skin tighter at his attention. "Yes. And I hate you. You hurt Neassa."

"Maybe I should take your skin from you." Mikhail threatened, not meaning his words at all.

A grip wrapped around his wrist, squeezing hard enough to hurt. Neassa's calm expression was frightening, though Mikhail did not recoil from her like he wanted to. His other hand wrapped around her wrist, holding her as she held him. She was close enough to kiss, her lips beckoning to him.

Pain flared in his side and Mikhail groaned, pulling away from the little selkie with the blade. She'd struck him deep. He released Nessa, touching his side tentatively. His palm came away slick and dark with blood. It was not too painful, but he needed to have it tended to quickly.

He turned, intending to head for the door and leave Neassa to deal with the angry girl. A stabbing pain in his chest made him stumble, using the bed for support. Neassa cried out behind him and he felt hands take hold of his arm. Her hands investigated, finding the warm blood that ran down his side.

"Niamh, you idiot." Neassa hissed. "I told you to leave him be!"

"You were never going to be free of him!" Niamh whined. "I wanted you to be happy."

"I cannot breathe." Mikhail murmured, holding onto Neassa.

Her hands touched his cheeks. "We will take you to the pools. Niamh, help me."

"I will not." Niamh huffed.

Neassa's hand connected with Niamh's face, knocking the girl back a few steps. Mikhail grabbed Neassa's hand as it lifted again, stopping her from continuing. He could not watch someone so young be beaten, no matter what they had done. Niamh's cheek had a bright red hand mark, and tears already streaked down her cheeks. Neassa pulled her arm from Mikhail's hold and turned to him again.

"Do not blame her." Mikhail murmured, wincing as

pain rushed across his chest again.

"Help me, Niamh." Neassa hissed.

The girl grabbed Mikhail roughly, his weight balanced between the two of them. He struggled to take a breath, pain beginning to radiate across his shoulder and back. Neassa's hand was on his stomach, keeping him upright as they began to shuffle from the room. Mikhail straightened, trying to walk on his own.

"Mikhail, you will hurt yourself." Neassa gasped.

"It does not matter." Mikhail groaned.

His voice was weak and raspy, it hurt to draw in breath. He could feel Neassa and Niamh against his sides again, holding him upright. Mikhail wanted nothing more than to sink to the floor and wait for the pain to end. He needed a wise one, one of the physicians, a well-trained soldier. Anyone to help the pain end.

"Where are we going?" Niamh asked, hissing her words over his head.

"To the pools." Neassa grunted. "Where we came in."

The pools... Mikhail tried to stand straight again, but he was beginning to feel dizzy. He needed more air. He shuffled along, the two women supporting him. The hallways looked different in the dark, haunting. Mikhail had never walked them without light. Darkness pressed in on him and his pain, narrowing his focus to the few paces he could see ahead of him. Even the moonlight did not pierce the shadows.

"We are nearly there, Mikhail." Neassa murmured to him. "Just stay with me. Do not leave me, please."

A door opened and closed and then there were echoes all around them. This place he knew. The light never reached the corners of this passageway. The rough stone had been worn smooth by hundreds of years of the royal family walking through the natural tunnel. He felt more at peace. He would die in the same place as his mother.

The darkness never left, pressing harder on Mikhail's eyes now. For him there was nothing to see. He held tighter to Neassa, fear starting to brush through his mind. Mikhail did not want to die. Even if he had to live with the pain for the rest of his life, he wanted to live. Her hands were soft and brushed through his hair and across his face. She whispered to him, in a tongue he did not recognise, but the sound gave him comfort.

"We are nearly there, Mikhail." Neassa murmured. Mikhail felt the stairs under his shaky feet. Water enveloped him, his hands grasping frantically at Neassa until she pressed her body against his. She was with him. Neassa would not let him drown. A new pain sparked in his side, the water stinging the wound that Niamh had left with her knife. Pain still radiated across his chest, still unable to draw a full breath. He could feel the side of the pool at his back.

"Try to relax, Mikhail." Neassa murmured. "I will ask the ocean to help."

"You should not." Niamh spat by his head. "I will tell the Council and you will get in trouble."

"I do not fear them." Neassa replied calmly. "You may leave. I will return home when he is whole again."

"I am not leaving you!"

"You have done enough damage!" Neassa shouted, her voice echoing darkly. "Leave, Niamh, before I tell the Council what *you* have done. You have broken more rules than I. I am cleaning up your mess."

Silence came again, Mikhail trying to draw breath. Neassa slipped from his hold for a moment, leaving him panicking in the water. When she returned, his hands found bare flesh, smooth and soft. She had removed her shawl. For a moment, Mikhail wished he could see the stunning beauty that he knew Neassa would have. Her hands eased his shirt over his head, their chests pressed tight together.

"Relax, Mikhail." Neassa whispered. "I am here. I will not let you die."

"Neassa... I am scared." Mikhail admitted.

Lips pressed against his, distracting him for a short time. Neassa pulled away too soon, Mikhail gasping for breath again. She began to speak, no, she was singing. The words were haunting, like the old ghosts that people claimed to hear on old battlefields. She was singing, power threaded through her words, power that Mikhail could not place. The pain slipped from his consciousness and Mikhail was floating in the wide ocean.

It was nighttime above him, the stars emblazoned across the sky. He had never felt such peace. The ocean cradled him, holding him up from its depths. There was no more pain, there was no more worry. His father was nowhere near, he was free. He could hear Neassa's voice, below him in the water. Mikhail wanted to keep watching the sky. He wanted to count the stars.

A gentle hand slipped up his arm, a dark shape just breaking the surface of the water. Neassa? Mikhail looked back to the stars, for one last look before he was drawn under the surface. He could not breathe here, but the dark shape did not seem to care.

Down, down, down, he was pulled, his lungs burning. He needed to breathe. Mikhail tried to free himself from the hold, but it was too strong. He was going to drown here, deep under the ocean. If only he could see the stars one last time. The dark shape kept pulling, drawing him down deeper and deeper.

"Mikhail!" Neassa shouted.

He sat up, coughing hard. Water splashed from his mouth into the pool. She was still pressed to his side, her heart beating rapidly in her chest. He could feel every inch of her skin that was pressed against him. Mikhail tried to release her, but she would not move away.

"We have to stay like this for a while longer." Neassa murmured. "Until I am sure that you are healed." Mikhail relaxed back against the edge of the pool, letting his breathing return to normal. "What did you do to me?"

"I am not sure. I asked the ocean to heal you." Neassa replied, her head resting on his shoulder. "It guided me, but I am not sure what happened. You stopped breathing."

"I was drowning." Mikhail whispered. "I was out on the ocean, under the stars. And then something dragged me under."

Neassa did not speak, leaving Mikhail to relive the dream again and again. It was unnerving, to know that he had nearly died because he had not fought hard enough against the being in the dream. Next time, he would be prepared. Next time he would not give up. He hoped there was not another time.

"Can you breathe now?" Neassa questioned.

"Yes." Mikhail said softly. "Thank you."

Her lips pressed against his cheek. "Do not thank me. It was because of me that you were hurt."

"Niamh... Who is she?" Mikhail asked.

"My sister."

"I cannot fault her for wanting me dead." He let out a sad chuckle. "I did break your heart. And yet you are here. You drew me back from death. Why?"

There was no answer for a long moment. "Because I do not want to be free of this bond."

Mikhail sighed.

"Do not misunderstand." Neassa started. "I do wish that you had not denied me. But the bond is something that none of my sisters have experienced. I can feel your heartbeat. I know when you are afraid, or angry, or happy."

Her hand touched his chest, laying over his heart. It felt right to have her hand on his skin. Mikhail wanted to draw her in for a deep kiss, but he could not. He would not give her false hope. He would not break her heart again. He would not draw her into the life that gave him so much pain.

"You are always so sad." Neassa whispered. "Except for right now. You feel at peace. That is why I know you did not want to drive me away."

"Neassa." Mikhail groaned. "Neassa, please."

She pressed a finger to his lips. "You were so afraid when you sent me away. I thought you were afraid of me. I am not asking to remain by your side. I know you will not allow it. But I wanted to know,... are you shielding me from something?"

"Yes." He answered shortly.

Neassa relaxed into his touch. There was silence, only the gentle lapping of the water to show the passage of time. Slowly, Mikhail began to stroke her hair, marvelling at the length that floated in the water around them. He wished he could see how she looked, naked and curled against him, with only her hair to protect her modesty. It was better that he did not.

"I should return to my chambers." Mikhail murmured. "And you should return to your people."

"Can we stay a little longer?" Neassa asked. "The dawn has not come yet."

"No. We should not remain in each other's company more than we need to." Mikhail pulled himself from the pool and away from Neassa.

"As you wish." Neassa's voice was filled with pain... and peace.

He found his shirt, still sodden, on the ground and tried to pull it over his head. There was a laugh and Neassa's hands guided the wet material into place. Mikhail kept his face blank, remembering that she could see in the dim light. Her hand touched his wrist and she drew him up the stairs to the door.

"Will you be able to reach the end without light?" She asked.

Mikhail considered lying for only a heartbeat. "Yes. I will be fine."

CHAPTER FIVE

"Mikhail, you are wet." Yordan's voice broke through his thoughts.

He stopped, his hand on his door handle. Yordan had been sitting on the floor, almost hidden in the dark hallway. Mikhail opened his room, gesturing for his brother to follow him inside. Sodden clothing was peeled from his frame, tossed aside to land in the corners of his room.

"Why are you not in your chambers with your wife?" Mikhail asked.

Yordan closed the door as he entered. "I do not want to talk about it."

Mikhail slammed his hands against the closet that held his clothing. "And I do." He shouted. "Why are you not with your wife? Why are you such a coward? She is one woman and you allow her to walk over you. Do you have no spine?"

"She is a princess from another country, I am giving

her respect." Yordan shouted back. "Do not tell me what I should be doing. You have not been sold off to make an alliance. You still have your freedom."

Turning, Mikhail drove his fist into Yordan's jaw. The younger man buckled under the unexpected attack and dropped to the floor. Mikhail regretted his actions, but his brother was being idiotic. He turned away, rubbing his face. How did his brother not understand that as the eldest, Mikhail would never be free. The marriage he entered into would be one to push the kingdom forward.

"There have been too many generations of our family marrying below our rank." Mikhail murmured. "You are not the only one who will have to marry someone of noble blood. At least your wife is a princess, who has some idea how to carry herself. I will be stuck with some noble girl, from a family who can buy the entire city twice over."

Yordan clambered back to his feet, eyes filled with tears. "She could have married you."

"Father would never allow a foreign brat on the throne." Mikhail spat, echoing his father's words. "He had no choice but to offer you so as not to offend their queen."

"It is not fair." Yordan muttered.

"Nothing is fair!" Mikhail rounded on his brother. "Nothing is fair in this life. You were born royalty. Your life is a gift. Would you rather have been born a peasant? To work every day of your life and never be sure if you will be able to feed your children?"

"I would rather their freedom."

"There is no freedom for them. They work until the day they die. They can leave, but wherever they go, there will be someone lording over them. They are still bound by laws. They are the first to die in wars and plagues."

"You know nothing about their lives. You are the same as me." Yordan hissed. "You cannot say you know what it is like to be one of them."

"Our lives are no more free than theirs. We have expectations that bind us. Traditions to uphold. We are here to serve them. To protect them. To not start wars for personal grudges where they will die." Mikhail sighed. "Our lives are a different kind of servitude."

"Father had never said anything like that before." Yordan scoffed. "Where are you pulling it from?"

Mikhail turned to his brother. "From Mother. That is the kind of king I want to be."

Guilt flashed over Yordan's face and he fell silent.

Mikhail returned to his task of dressing himself, pulling a fresh tunic over his head. Their mother had always whispered in his ear, telling him that those were the reasons he was born a prince. Not to rise greater than anyone else, but to serve his country with his life. Just as a soldier would. Just as a humble farmer. His task was no more important than theirs.

"Mother never told me anything like that." Yordan murmured.

"You were still young when she passed." Mikhail replied. "She was trying to wash away some of Father's arrogance."

Yordan scuffed his foot against the rug. "Kismet terrifies me." He admitted softly. "She is always watching. Even in the night, if I turn to face her, she is already watching me."

"You will have to put a baby in her belly soon." Mikhail sighed. "Father is angry with both of you. She is not following the terms of the alliance."

"I will not force her, Mikhail."

He laughed. "I am not saying you should. That would cause many more problems than we already have. You need to talk to her."

The doors to his room opened, Kismet standing in the doorway. The gown she wore was covered in pearl beads, making her glimmer as she turned. Mikhail and Yordan bowed together, earning a short laugh from Kismet. It was the first sound of joy Mikhail had heard from her.

"For a moment, I thought I was home." Kismet said. "To see you both bow to me. But then I remembered that is the manners of your kingdom."

She stepped forward, closing the doors behind her. Mikhail would have protested the action had he gotten any sleep that night. For now he did not care if anyone had seen her enter his rooms. Yordan was here with him, and rumours could be easily ended. He sighed, offering a seat to the princess.

"To what do I owe the honour of having you visit me?" Mikhail asked as Kismet sat.

"I was looking for him." Kismet waved her hand to Yordan. "And you."

Mikhail sat on his bed, leaning against the frame in a rare show of laziness. "Continue, then. What is it you need?"

Kismet frowned, leaning forward in her seat to peer at Mikhail's crotch. He shifted, uncomfortable with her gaze and glanced down. Blood had splashed against the blankets in the night, a dried spot of dark brown now marred the colour.

"Why is there blood?" Kismet asked, standing quickly.

Her eyes darted across the room, noting the tiny trail that led to his door. An instant later she had a blade in her hand, a delicate thing that had appeared from seemingly nowhere. Yordan jumped to his feet, peering around the room with his wife.

"Please, relax." Mikhail groaned. "It is nothing."

"Were you attacked?" Yordan snapped.

"No!" Mikhail yelled. "Sit down both of you."

The blade never left Kismet's hand as she lowered herself slowly back into her seat. In normal circumstances, Mikhail might have been impressed by the thin blade. But there was no time to admire it. Kismet was the kind of princess that would know how to use the blade, Mikhail could sense it.

"I had a visitor last night." Mikhail murmured. "Of the female kind. We may have gotten slightly overzealous in our activities."

"Liar." Kismet snarled. "I have been here a week and already I know you would never have had a female visitor. It seems to be your one positive quality."

Mikhail shot a glare to Yordan. "Perhaps I am very discreet."

"Rumours would spread." Kismet shook her head. "No matter how discreet. Either girls would go missing, or there would be the softest whispers in dark corners about your conquests."

Yordan stood, offering a hand to Kismet. "Shall we just follow the blood trail?"

Mikhail watched surprise cross Kismet's face before the expression turned into a dazzling smile. Her hand was laid into Yordan's and she stood, leaving her hand in his. That was an interesting development. For a moment he considered allowing them to leave without opposition.

"It does not lead anywhere." Mikhail muttered, stepping between them and the door. "Though I am very amused by your ability to join forces to irritate me. Leave it be."

"No." Kismet smiled. "Come, Yordan. With you, I will be able to go anywhere in the castle."

He held the door shut, watching Kismet's smile turn to a frown. She still held the blade in her hand. If she turned it on him, he could throw her in a dungeon somewhere until she decided that she would behave. Yordan could join her until he had the servants clean up the blood trail.

"I will tell Father." Yordan spoke.

His gaze snapped to his brother. "Do not."

"Ah, so it is something that he would be interested in." Yordan grinned. "If you tell us, or let us follow the trail, I will keep it to myself."

"You will not... Just..." Mikhail fumbled for some reason for them to avoid the trail. "It does not concern you."

Yordan's eyes widened. "You were in the pools. That is why your clothing was wet."

Yordan grabbed Kismet's hand tightly and shoved their way through the doors, Mikhail being knocked to the side. He could hear Yordan telling Kismet to run and the sounds of their steps racing away.

Exhaustion washed over him, robbing him of his strength. He sat down slowly, giving up on chasing his brother. There was nothing he could do to persuade the younger man from his thoughts.

Mikhail laid back on his bed, wishing the door would close themselves so he could sleep. No servants wandered the halls yet, it was too early for him to yell at a passing girl to close his door for him. The dawn was finally breaking, golden light drifting across his ceiling. He wondered what Neassa was doing. His fingers crept under his tunic to touch the new scar just below his ribs.

What would they find in the pools, Mikhail wondered. Would they find evidence of blood, signs that would point to Neassa's presence. Had she left clothing behind? Had she been wearing anything more than her shawl? Mikhail could not remember. He could remember her soft skin against his. He groaned, rolling onto his side and staring out his window.

She had said that she could feel his emotions through their bond. Would he be able to do the same with her? Mikhail sighed. It would be a torture, to know what Neassa was feeling. To remember her lips on his. He buried his face into his pillow, breathing deeply and trying to calm himself. Distractions would not help at a time like this.

He thought of her face, the gentle smile she had given him when they had first met. The strong expression she had worn when she spoke to the king made him chuckle. She was like a warrior, fierce and unrelenting. Even though he had pushed her away, she would not give up on their bond. He wanted to hold her again.

Mikhail sat up, dragging himself from his bed to close the doors firmly. He was alone now. In the small room where he had nearly died. He could smell Neassa on his blankets, the fresh scent of the ocean. He pulled the blankets to his face, breathing in deeply. He wished to tuck his face against her neck, to feel her fingers through his hair. He did not want to be alone.

But he had spoken the truth to Yordan, his life was not free, he could not choose her. He would not choose her. He had already seen the pressure of their lives wear down their mother. He could not bear for it to happen to Neassa also. Mikhail desperately wished for sleep, for the sweet nothingness. If only sleep would take him from his thoughts.

"Mikhail!" Yordan slammed the doors open. "You were in the pools. There was so much blood. What happened?"

"Do not shout." Mikhail growled, sitting up to see them both standing in the doorway. "Close the door before you start speaking."

Kismet stepped forward as Yordan shut the door, staring at him with fear and worry. What had she thought of the hidden pools? What did she think had happened to him? He remembered the pain of breathing. If not for Neassa, he would have died. Niamh's furious face flashed into his mind. He had been wrong to hurt Neassa so much.

"Are you crying?" Kismet asked softly.

"Yes." Mikhail answered, burying his face into his blanket.

There was silence as he wept, the pitiful sound filling the room. Someone's arms wrapped around him, holding him and Mikhail allowed it. It was a long time before he lifted his head again, eyes stinging from the tears. Kismet pulled herself from him, giving him a slight smile. Yordan was watching from the corner of the room, eyes dark with jealousy.

"What happened last night?" Yordan growled.

Mikhail lifted his tunic, touching the new scar that marred his abdomen. "I was stabbed."

Yordan came closer. "It is old."

"It was new, before I went to the pools." Mikhail murmured. "I do not know where to start."

"Does it have anything to do with the woman who appeared, claiming to be your bride?" Kismet questioned.

"What?" Yordan gasped.

"How do you know about that?" Mikhail asked.

Kismet smiled, an expression filled with mischief. "A woman hears many things."

There had been many in the throne room when Neassa had first appeared. Of course some of them had spoken of the strange woman. Mikhail sighed. The king would not be happy if he heard the rumours had spread. He ran his fingers through his hair, pushing the locks back from his face.

"Yes." He answered.

"Did she stab you?" Yordan asked.

Anger flashed through Mikhail. "No. She would never do that."

Yordan sighed. "Do not snap at me, brother."

Kismet slipped between them. "Stop fighting like children. If you do not tell us what happened, then we make assumptions, Mikhail. You are just like my brothers. Both of you."

"Her sister came to kill me." Mikhail answered through clenched teeth.

Yordan jerked in the corner, standing up straight. "Why?"

He looked out the window where he could see the ocean. Neassa would be there now, hopefully swimming peacefully with her sister by her side. Mikhail never wanted to disrupt her life, he did not want it to be affected by him. He wanted her to be safe and happy, always.

53

"Do you know about creatures called selkies?" Mikhail asked softly.

CHAPTER SIX

Mikhail set down his lantern. The light caught on the surface of the water, sending a long line out into the dark. His chest had been bothering him for most of the day. He had finally been dismissed by his father and sought refuge in the pool caverns. It was silent, without the disturbance of Yordan and Kismet.

The two of them had been surprised by his revelation of Neassa's existence. Kismet had asked many questions about her, but would give no reason why she was so interested. Mikhail worried about that. Yordan had been irritated, complaining that it was not fair that Mikhail was attempting to avoid his duty to the crown. It had not taken Kismet much to force him to agree that Mikhail had not chosen Neassa and the situation he was in.

His father would not speak of the selkie girl that had come to his throne room nearly a month ago, and Mikhail could not keep her from his mind. Perhaps it was because she was the first woman he had allowed to get close to him. He could still feel her lips on his when he remembered that night.

He had not heard anything from her. Yordan and Kismet had been spending more time together since he had shared his tale. Perhaps there would be a child soon. It would be a welcome distraction. The king had been aggressive in his attempts to push Mikhail into marriage. He was not enjoying the attention.

Slowly, Mikhail stripped off his clothes and slipped into the cool water. The water embraced him, his body floating easily on the surface. He could hear gentle lapping. It soothed him, drawing away his worries. Mikhail wondered if Neassa could feel his calm through their bond.

"Would it work for me?" He asked out loud, his voice muffled by the water that covered his ears. He closed his eyes, blocking out the light from the lantern and brought Neassa's smile to his mind. Her expression quickly changed to the heartbroken look she had given him the first time they had met. Mikhail gasped, floundering in the water. He struggled to push Neassa's pain from his mind.

His hands pressed against his eyes. That look haunted him. He wanted nothing more than to forget how he had hurt her, how he was still hurting her. Swimming to the edge, Mikhail hauled himself out of the water. Perhaps it was a mistake to come here again. He had avoided this place since his mother's death. Some part of him was sure his mother's spirit still soaked in the pool. It felt as though she was disappointed in him.

Bringing his knees to his chest, Mikhail wrapped his

arms around his legs. He missed his mother, more than he would ever admit to anyone. It was becoming difficult to remember her voice, and the way she would laugh at his silly questions. She had always found a chance to hold them, even when they grew old enough to claim embarrassment from her affection.

There was nothing he wanted more than to feel his mother's arms around him again. To feel her gentle fingers stroke through his hair like he was a child once more. He wanted to apologise for distancing himself when she was sick. Simply, Mikhail wanted his mother. Tears stung his eyes and, for the first time in years, he did not force away the sorrow.

His sobs echoed back to him, drowning him with the sounds of his grief. Without the queen, the king had become hard and angry. Mikhail had also. Mocking his brother for his mourning, as if he had felt nothing when their mother died. But, just as Mikhail had begun to unravel his grief, Yordan had come back from his journey, sobbing about a mountain girl that had gotten killed.

With his brother in mourning, again, Mikhail had forced his own grief away, to shield his brother from their father's anger. But he wanted to be weak. He wanted to cry and be held and be the one protected from their father. There had been no one to do that for him. When Neassa had appeared, he thought that perhaps his wish had been granted.

If Neassa had not been a selkie, Mikhail wondered if he would have been allowed to marry her. The king had married a commoner and the realm had not suffered for it. As had their grandfather. So many of their family line had plucked peasant girls from their lives of poverty and dressed them as queens. Would Mikhail have been allowed to do the same?

He buried his face in his knees, taking long shaky breaths as his sobbing slowly calmed. There was no use to sitting in the dark and crying about his fate. Mikhail started to pack away his grief. His brother would most likely be looking for him again. He was never allowed a moment's peace, but it kept his heart from breaking.

Mikhail dressed himself slowly, finding that the pain in his chest had eased. Neassa had been right, the ocean water did have some magic. He passed the pool that his mother had bathed in, his gaze lingering on the smooth edge that she had sat against. She had spent so much time in this dark place, but she had been happy, he thought.

Light swung wildly through the cavern. Mikhail turned, squinting towards the entrance. He could not see who it was until they turned their lantern away, his eyes struggling to adjust. Yordan's face appeared in the sunspots the lantern had left in his vision. His brother was crying.

"Yordan?"

There was no answer. Yordan slowly walked towards him, lantern hanging in his limp grip. Once he was close enough, Mikhail took the lantern from his brother and set it on the ground. What had happened to make him so upset.

"Where is Kismet?" He asked, suddenly fearful that something had happened to her.

Yordan shook his head. "It is not her."

A black hole opened up under Mikhail and he felt his heart falling. Their father. It was the only person that Yordan would find him for. His hands tightened on

Yordan's shoulders and he began to shake his
brother. It was aggressive and angry, his fingers
digging into his brother's flesh. Trying to spill the
news from his brother.

"Mikhail." Yordan sobbed, unresisting. "Mikhail, he
is gone."

His fingers released his brother's shoulders and
Mikhail's arms wrapped around his brother, drawing
the younger man into a hug. Hot tears soaked into his
shirt and rolled over his skin. He could feel tears
stinging at his eyes and squeezed them shut. Yordan
needed him to be strong. Without his strength,
Yordan would crumble. He would mourn later.

"Show me." Mikhail said gently.

Yordan pulled from his embrace, shuffling to the arch
that led to the long passageway. The silence pressed
down on Mikhail as they walked, the light from their
lantern pooling at their feet. With Yordan's shuffling
steps, it took them longer than Mikhail had thought
to reach the door into the castle proper.

Kismet was waiting by the door, her face a calm mask.
Her hands were clasped neatly in front of her, the
picture of perfect nobility. Mikhail could see pain in
her eyes as their gazes met. He gave a slight nod,
straightening his shoulders and pushing down his
emotions. With Kismet as witness, Mikhail could not
break apart.

"The king is in his chambers." Kismet murmured.
"He would be readying for sleep at this time."

Mikhail nodded, guiding the still silent Yordan
through the hallways. "He was old. We knew this
would come. Though we did not think it would be so
soon."

Surprising him, Kismet came to Yordan's side, taking

his hand gently. They had grown closer than Mikhail had thought. He was glad that Yordan had someone to comfort him. The younger man would need it in the coming weeks.

"Oh." Mikhail whispered to himself.

"What?" Kismet asked, peering at him closely. "What is wrong?"

"If Father is gone..." Mikhail stopped, shaking the thought from his head. "It does not matter. Let us go to him."

Servants were gathered in the hallways, their eyes wide with worry. When they saw Mikhail, they began to melt away, scurrying back to their tasks. He did not blame them for being curious. His father had been strong for a man of his age. It was a shock that he had died.

Drawing in a deep breath, Mikhail opened the door to his father's chambers and stepped inside. A healer lifted his gaze from the king's still form and bowed low. Mikhail gave the wise one a slight nod and approached the bed.

His father looked so much smaller. It was as if he had shrunk, leaving behind a mere prune of a man. Mikhail took his father's hand then dropped it instantly. It was cold to the touch, and the fingers struggled to bend in his hand. Armo, the healer, gave him a sympathetic look.

"Forgive me for not warning you, Prince Mikhail. It is not a pleasant feeling." The man murmured.

"Is this normal?" Mikhail asked.

Armo nodded. "In all dead things. He did not suffer. He had called for me, and in the time it took the servant to find me and bring me to him, he had passed on. The guards reported no shouts or sounds of pain. I believe he simply slipped into a slumber."

"At least he did not suffer." Kismet murmured from behind him.

"Were there signs that he was growing weak, Armo?" Mikhail asked.

"No." The healer sighed. "The king has been resistant to care, since the queen passed. I suspect he wished to join her."

"He did." Mikhail confirmed, sitting on the edge of his father's bed. "But he would not take his own life."

"It is a coward's end." Yordan murmured. "That is what he always said."

"I cannot say if he was right or wrong." Armo spread his hands. "I will leave you with him. I imagine you wish to say goodbye."

Mikhail nodded. The healer bowed low to all of them and stepped from the room. As the door closed, Mikhail heard Armo's calm voice tell the servants to go back to their tasks, that what had passed was done and their lingering at the door would change nothing. The door clicked shut and left them in silence.

"What will we do?" Yordan asked. "He is dead."

"We will do as tradition dictates." Mikhail murmured. "I cannot take the throne as king until I marry. I will choose one of the noble girls and we will be married after the mourning."

"What of..." Kismet hesitated. "Neassa?"

Pain flashed in Mikhail's heart. How he longed to call for her. To feel her arms around him in comfort. He closed his eyes, banishing the thoughts from his mind. She would not thrive in this life. Neassa belonged with the sea, to swim freely where she wished. The life of royalty would cage her.

"You will not speak her name again." Mikhail said

evenly. "She is not your concern."

Deep concern flashed over Kismet's face, but Mikhail chose to ignore her expression. Yordan was weeping silently, his shoulders hunched forward. His brother would be no use to him in that state. There was much to organise, many of his father's tasks would be left to him while his brother mourned.

"Kismet. Take Yordan and..." Mikhail waved his hand.

"I will take care of him." Kismet assured him, slipping her hand into her husband's and leading him from the room.

Mikhail was left alone. He slumped into a seat, staring at the king's lifeless body. Death had touched their family again. It should have been unsurprising with the king's age, but it was a heavy blow to Mikhail's heart. Burying his face in his hands, Mikhail struggled not to cry. Now, more than ever, Mikhail wished his mother was still alive.

"May I enter, Prince Mikhail?"

His hands dropped from his face, shocked by how dark the room had grown. How long had he been sitting there in the dark. Mikhail looked to the door where the wise one stood at the door, his face arranged in a gentle smile.

"Of course, Armo." He murmured.

The white haired man stepped into the room and closed the door behind him. He made no movement beyond the doorway, his hands hidden by the long sleeves he wore. Mikhail sighed deeply. Armo had been treating their family since he was a child. He was a familiar face around their court.

"I see Prince Yordan has left." Armo observed. Mikhail nodded.

"Do you wish someone to talk to?"

"Whether I talk or not, it will not change things." Mikhail murmured.

Armo gave a slight smile. "Perhaps. But it will lighten the load on your heart, would it not? I asked you the same thing when your mother died. You refused me then, and you have been carrying her death with you all this time. Are you going to do the same with your father?"

"I don't believe even the Wise Ones can question a king." Mikhail muttered, rubbing his face.

"I believe that we may offer advice without fear of punishment." Armo corrected. "You sent your brother away to mourn. That was a wise decision." Mikhail looked at the dead king. "I do not know how to plan a funeral for a king."

"No one ever does." Armo moved to the fireplace, arranging the kindling. "The king was caught unprepared when his father died also."

"Where is your apprentice?" Mikhail asked suddenly, realising that the wise one's living shadow had not been seen.

Armo glanced at the door. "While I tend to death here, she tends to life. There is a babe being born in another part of the castle."

He could hold his mask no longer, the sorrow and despair he had been holding back finally breaking through. Mikhail began to sob, the sound of his deep gasping breaths filling the room. His face buried into his hands, rocking in his chair. He did not want to be king. He did not want to rule over the people.

A strong hand touched his shoulder and he lifted his head to look up at Armo. The man's face was grave. Mikhail dropped his head back to his hands and continued sobbing. It was only a few moments before the hand left his shoulder and Mikhail heard the door to the room open and close. He could not move, he could not do anything but sit and weep. For his mother, for his father, for himself, and for Neassa. His tears dried, long after the sun had set and the stars had emerged. Exhaustion washed over him, and Mikhail leaned back in the chair, staring at the ceiling. He felt empty. As though all of his emotions had been poured out of him with the tears. Mikhail grasped at the lack of feeling and let it fill him. There was much he had to do before he could take the throne.

"Prince Mikhail." A voice addressed him.

Mikhail rolled his head over to see who it was that spoke. Armo was standing in the doorway again, a mug in his hands. It was steaming. He could not draw his eyes from the lazy tendril of steam that drifted upwards. Realising he had not responded, Mikhail cleared his throat.

"Wise One." He mumbled, unable to bring back the firmness of his voice. "Is that for me?"

"It is." Armo replied. "A tea to help you sleep. I suggest drinking this and then heading to your chambers. The king will be attended to through the night. You need rest. It has been a heavy night for all."

Pushing himself up from the chair, Mikhail felt only slight alarm as his balance nearly pitched him to the floor. He felt weak, as if the tears he had shed carried his strength away as well as his emotions. Armo pressed the warm cup to his hands. Mikhail drained it in three big gulps and sighed. He recognised the tea. It was the same one he had taken when his mother died.

"The guards will escort you to your room." Armo murmured, leading him to the door. "Rest well, Prince Mikhail. You need your strength."

He was not sure how he got to his rooms, only that he was there. The bed beckoned to him and Mikhail did not even bother to remove his clothes before he collapsed into its softness. Tears came to his eyes again, and he did not try to fight them back. He slipped into sleep, the tea working quickly in his fragile state.

CHAPTER SEVEN

Mikhail came awake slowly. The blanket was cool against his bare back, and his feet had been freed from his boots. There was warmth under him and his arms tightened around the slender figure. Gentle fingers stroked through his hair softly, almost lulling him back to sleep with the soothing caress.

He came fully awake, pushing himself up off the woman he had been resting against. A small sound of surprise came from her as he moved. His eyes struggled to focus, the sleeping tea still having a hold over him. Neassa stared up at him from the pillows, a slight smile on her face now.

She was not really here, not in his bed, not with that sweet smile. Mikhail trembled, sure that he was hallucinating. There was no way she could ignore the pain he had caused her. Neassa's fingers lifted and stroked over his face and down his bare chest. He relaxed, burying his face back into her dress. Her fingers returned to the gentle stroking through his hair.

"Why are you here?" Mikhail mumbled against her.

"I felt your heart breaking." She whispered.

Her heartbeat was slow and steady. He clung to her, pressing his face into the simple dress that covered her frame. She kept stroking his hair, not asking anything from him. Mikhail could feel tears stinging his eyes and he tried to hold them back. He could not cry in front of her, she would think less of him for it.

"Mikhail." Neassa murmured. "You can cry."

Lifting his head, Mikhail met Neassa's eyes. He searched for disgust or pity in her expression but found none. There was pain in her eyes, and he realised the pain was for him. His eyes stung and he pressed his face to her chest again, shoulders trembling as he tried not to cry.

Her fingers did not stop in their gentle stroking and, quite unwillingly, Mikhail began to sob against her. She whispered softly, her words lost under the noise of his tears. He clutched at her tighter, drawing a slight hitch in her breath. Mikhail knew he must be crushing her ribs, but he could not bring himself to loosen his grasp. If he released her, she would leave and not return.

Neassa did not try to break free, her hands still combing softly through his hair. Her dress became damp under his face as his tears soaked into the material. Surely now she would pull away. She would be disgusted in his show of emotion and ask to be free of his hold. But she did not. Still she did not. Mikhail continued to cry, believing that in just a few more seconds, a few more moments, Neassa would ask for her freedom.

Mikhail's tears slowly dried. He tried to pull away from Neassa but her arms tightened around him, keeping him close. Lifting his head, Mikhail found that Neassa had been crying too, her cheeks damp with tears. Reaching out a shaking hand, he wiped them from her skin. The tiny smile on her face, framed with tears that still fell, was heartbreaking.

"Neassa." Mikhail whispered.

"I am alright." She murmured back. "I am glad that you allowed me to stay. Thank you. I wanted to comfort you."

He shifted his weight, bringing his face up to hers. Their lips met in a gentle kiss. But it did not stay gentle for long. Mikhail's hand tangled in Neassa's hair at the base of her skull. She pressed her lips against his more firmly. There was a mindless desperation in their movements as Mikhail lay over her, using his weight to hold her down.

"Mikhail." Neassa breathed.

Groaning softly, Mikhail tried to stop. His body betrayed him, drawn in by the warmth of Neasa's body. He wanted nothing more than to take Neassa in that moment. And she was willing, he could tell by the way she arched her back so that her breasts pressed against his chest. Mikhail wanted her, and he did not have the strength to stop himself.

"I need you." He admitted softly. "I want more than innocent comfort."

A sweet smile passed over Neassa's face. "You have me. All of me."

He groaned again, his head dropping to her shoulder. She was a temptress. Mikhail wanted to pull away, wanted to leave the room and calm himself. But

Neassa's arms were around him and she was much stronger than she appeared. Gently, Mikhail began to leave soft kisses over her neck and shoulder, trying to ground himself. He just needed a moment, he thought, just a moment and then he would pull away. His kisses began to trail lower, following the line of her clothing. It was frustrating that he could go no lower. He wanted to see her lying beneath him, calling him to her with her smile. Mikhail sighed against her skin. A few more moments, a few more kisses, and then he would pull away. A little longer in her arms and then Mikhail would be satisfied.

She writhed under him, Mikhail lifted his head for a moment to give her a questioning look. Neassa gave a sly smile and then, before Mikhail could stop her, she had released herself of her dress, pulling it up over her head and tossing it aside. He let out a long breath, staring down at the vision he had been granted. His strength broke.

His mouth found her breasts again, kissing over the warm mounds. His tongue flicked out over the little hard tip, drawing a happy gasp from Neassa. Mikhail did it again, delighting in the way she shifted, trying to pull him tighter against her. He had to control himself, or he would go too far. Neassa whimpered under him as he continued to kiss at her breasts, teasing her with only the softest of touches. It was a beautiful sound.

How long he spent exploring the soft mounds and valley of her chest he could not have said, but eventually, he traced a line of kisses back to her lips. She welcomed him back with a soft kiss, her fingers playing with his hair once more. Mikhail relaxed into her touch, pressing his lips along her jaw then down her neck again. He was delighted by the soft sighs and moans that Neassa let out as he explored.

He hesitated, now, unsure how to move forward. Neassa shifted under him, casting a curious look over his face. Again he remembered that she could feel his emotions. She must have felt the embarrassment and hesitation. Mikhail buried his face into her neck so she could not see him.

"I have never done this before." He murmured against her skin.

"Never?" She asked.

Mikhail shook his head. "Have you?"

Neassa gave a soft laugh. "Never. I was always bound to you, Mikhail. I would never let another touch me like this."

"Maybe that is why I never had the desire to lie with anyone before." Mikhail murmured against her skin.

"You were never tempted?"

Mikhail kissed her neck again. "No."

Sighing softly, Mikhail sat back on his heels, drinking in the sight of Neassa's nude form. Her skin was perfect and unmarred. Except for a series of silver scars on her right hip. Mikhail ran his thumb over them lightly, curious as to how they had gotten on her skin. He would ask later, for his gaze had been captured by other features.

Her legs were parted slightly, his kneeling form stopping her from closing them. She started to fidget then, unable to look at him as he studied her. Mikhail ran his thumb down her stomach to the smooth mound between her legs. She was smooth where other women were not.

Mikhail flushed, realising he had been staring. "It is beautiful."

"You are sure?" Neassa whispered.

"Yes."

He wanted to continue to explore her with his fingers, to follow the damp warmth that was emanating from between her legs. Neassa shifted suddenly, sitting up and hiding from his gaze. Her eyes lifted to his, only meeting his gaze for a few seconds before she looked away again.

"I am sorry. I did not mean to stare." Mikhail breathed, resting his weight on his hands to lean forward and kiss her. "I will join you."

Rather than struggling amongst the blankets, Mikhail stepped off the bed, fumbling with his clothing and letting his pants drop to the floor. He felt her embarrassment for himself as her eyes dropped to his manhood. Mikhail felt the need to cover himself and slipped back into the bed beside Neassa, using the blankets to hide. She flipped them back, her fingers caressing down his front.

"Can I touch it?" Neassa asked softly.

Not trusting himself to talk, Mikhail guided her hand to his shaft, wrapping it around himself. Neassa let out a soft noise, their hands moving together. She shifted forward, so she did not have to reach so far. Mikhail ran his hand up and down her back, marvelling at her warmth. Anything to distract himself from her gentle touch.

Finally, Mikhail could take it no longer and rolled, pushing Neassa to her back. Now that he had her spread below him again, he hesitated. Would it be right to take her and then still not allow her to stay by his side? It would be cruel. He began to pull back, unsure how to tell her that he could not.

Neassa's legs wrapped around his hips and she pulled

herself close, pressing her heat against his manhood. Mikhail closed his eyes, desperately trying to maintain his willpower. He could not do this to her. Then her words echoed in his head. She would never let another touch her like this. Slowly, carefully, Mikhail guided his tip to her, both letting out a soft noise. She may never be able to stay with him, but he could give her something to remember. Mikhail thrust forward, sinking into her heat. Neassa whined softly, her fingers gripping his shoulders. Her legs tightened around his hips and she pulled herself tighter to him until he was fully inside her.

"If it hurts, do not force yourself." Mikhail groaned, trying to remember what he knew of a woman's first time.

"It does not." Neassa murmured. "It does not hurt, Mikhail. Please, keep going."

With her urging, Mikhail began to explore her. They explored each other with their lips and hands as Mikhail gently rocked against her. It was not long before Mikhail found his release, his seed spilling into Neassa's depths. He was ashamed, he felt like a young boy. Neassa laughed softly, the merry sound hurting more.

"I am sorry. I did not mean to laugh." Neassa said quickly. "Your embarrassment was sweet. I do not mind, Mikhail. We have more time."

Mikhail shook his head. "I am sorry, I wanted to be better."

"No, do not pull out!" Neassa gasped, clutching him tightly. "Just stay like this a while."

"If that is what you want." Mikhail murmured.

Neassa played with his hair. "It is."

He kissed at her skin again, following the gentle lines

of her neck and shoulders. She returned the kisses often, her hands still tangled in his hair. Mikhail rested his weight on one arm, his other making gentle caresses up and down her sides. He felt a patch of roughness and remembered her scars.

"How did you get these?" He asked.

She glanced down. "I had almost forgotten. I got caught in a fisherman's net once. When he drew me up, I struggled, trying to free myself without having to change. I was thrashing so much that I did not see he was trying to help. His knife caught my hip as he tried to cut the net. I thought it was attacking me and panicked. He was not quick enough in pulling the knife away."

He lifted his fingers to his lips and kissed them before pressing them to her scars. Neassa laughed softly, nestling into the pillow under her head. Her eyes roamed his body and Mikhail hoped she would not ask about the scars on his arm. She touched them lightly.

"Can I ask?" Neassa murmured. "You got tense when I noticed them."

Sighing softly, Mikhail ran his fingers over her cheek. "Yordan was in trouble... for something, I do not even remember. It was just after Mother had passed. Father went to hit him and I jumped between them. I fell, and broke a crystal vase that had been Mother's. It took the Wise One hours to pull all the shards from my arm."

Neassa lifted his arm and pressed her lips to the silvery marks. "I am sorry."

"Do not be. I was protecting my brother." Mikhail smiled. "I will never regret doing that. But tell me, what happened here?"

He touched the silver spot under her eye. Neassa's cheek reddened and she pulled her cheek from his touch. She seemed embarrassed, rather than afraid, and Mikhail leaned down to press soft kisses over her cheeks.

"I will tell you!" Neassa laughed. "When I was young, I went to explore the reef that sits outside the harbour. I had never been there before, and the colours and animals, everything was amazing. I found an urchin. And, rather than leave it be, as my mother told me to, I began playing with it. One of its spines caught me just below the eye."

Mikhail chuckled softly. "That is not what I was expecting."

"Well I live most of my life in my seal form." Neassa explained. "What did you expect? It is easier that way."

He kissed her quickly, gazing down at her face. "I do not know. You seem much more civilised than one might expect from a wild animal."

"That is rude." She laughed. "We learn much from our neighbours. There are some of us who cannot change at all, our blood too diluted. They live near the docks, and that is where we claim to live when we walk among the people. It is sad for them, they can feel the call of the sea, but they cannot answer."

Mikhail touched her breast, running his hands over the smooth skin. "How does your blood become diluted?"

"Mating with you." Neassa answered. "Your people, not other selkies. We... have very few males born. And those that are... find themselves surrounded by willing women. My brother has twelve wives. He comes to me often to complain."

74

"Twelve?" Mikhail echoed. "That must be..."

"Difficult." She nodded. "They know how important he is and they love each other like sisters. But he has not had a son yet. And my sisters will likely never have selkie children."

Mikhail ran his thumb across her skin. "And what of you?"

It was a long moment before Neassa replied. "I do not expect that I will have any children. Of any kind."

Pain lanced through Mikhail's heart and he bowed his head. He was hurting Neassa again, simply by not asking her to stay. He could not. He would not take her from the sea. Mikhail let out a heavy sigh and was surprised when Neassa pressed her lips to his.

"I am happy just to be with you now." Her hips rolled slightly. "I can feel you inside me again. Will you..."

He silenced her with a firm kiss, her arms looping around him as he pinned her again under his weight. She was still slick as he began to move again. With her soft moans, she encouraged him to move more firmly against her. Mikhail fell into a rhythm, pressing his face to her shoulder.

This time, Mikhail controlled himself, focusing on the way Neassa gasped and moaned. Slowly but surely, they both came undone, together this time. Once more Mikhail spilled his seed inside of Neassa, her lips finding his for a long, drawn out kiss. Mikhail collapsed against her, unable to hold his weight and her arms held him close.

"I love you."

CHAPTER EIGHT

Mikhail woke before dawn, staring up at the ceiling above him. He half expected Neassa to be lying beside him, but his bed was empty. She had visited the last two nights, sneaking into his castle to see him. They had indulged in wordless exploration of each other's bodies, something Mikhail could not imagine doing with anyone else. They had shared stories of their childhoods. Growing closer as they learned more of each other's lives.

He swung his legs out of bed and stood, crossing to the window to look down the cliffs. Neassa would be there somewhere. There was a flash of guilt. He had probably woken her from her sleep when he had risen. If he could return to sleep and let her rest, he would. But today, he was saying farewell to his father. There would be no more sleep for him this morning. Rubbing his hands over his face, Mikhail tried to rouse himself fully. He turned away from the window, shuffling to the other room to relieve himself. The servants had not been yet. Clothes for the day had not been lain out. And his breakfast had not been brought. Mikhail considered going in search of food.

"Brother?" Yordan called through his door.

"If you have come to tell me that you and Kismet are fighting again, I refuse to listen." Mikhail snapped.

There was a slight chuckle. "So irritated this morning, brother. Did you not sleep well?"

Yordan shot him a grin as Mikhail opened the door to admit his brother. Mikhail did not have an answering smile, glancing at the bed as he searched for some clothing to pull on. He was not in the mood to suffer his brother's joyfulness. Not on this day.

"Why are you here, Yordan?" Mikhail sighed. "And why are you so happy. Or have you forgotten th-"

"I have forgotten nothing." Yordan broke in. "I am here because Kismet wanted time to ready herself. I am here because you are my brother. You were closer with Father than I was."

"That was not by choice."

"Neither was mine. Calm yourself, brother."

There was a hesitant knock on the door and Mikhail called for them to enter. Seija's face peered through the door and, when she found their eyes on her, she stepped forward confidently. She gave a quick bow before her chin lifted proudly, glancing between them.

"Wise One Seija." Yordan greeted happily. "I have not seen you in some time."

"I have not yet earned that title, Prince Yordan, but you flatter me. I have been tending to other things." She replied, her tone light and easy. "I am here in Armo's place. To ready Prince Mikhail."

Mikhail pushed Yordan's shoulder lightly. "You should return to your wife."

"You should find a wife." Yordan grinned, ducking under Mikhail's swipe. "I shall see you when we begin the march."

The doors closed behind him, leaving Seija and Mikhail alone. Armo's apprentice appraised him silently. Mikhail studied her in return. She wore the white robes of a Wise One, though hers were hemmed with green ribbon, to denote her apprenticeship. They were a sign of her removal from normal life.

"Are you ready to farewell your father?" She asked, breaking the silence.

Mikhail shook his head.

Seija sighed. "It is not easy. It never is. I have witnessed many funerals and the emotions of those saying farewell are always heavy. I can prepare a tea to dull the pain, if that is what you wish."

"No. I have done my mourning. I am ready to put the king to rest." Mikhail glanced over her again. "Why is Armo not here?"

Seija considered the question. "This is one of the few things that no Wise One can train for. The death of a monarch. It is a good lesson for me."

"A lesson?" Mikhail growled. "My father's death is a lesson to you?"

He rounded on the girl, towering over her, his anger bubbling in his chest. She stared up at him, unafraid. Seija did not step back, did not turn away, or raise her hands in defense. Mikhail stepped back, pressing his hands to his face. He had threatened a wise one, a mere slip of a girl.

"It is." Seija answered finally. "For the first time in

78

generations, we do not have a king to step into the throne. You are unmarried, still a prince, with no one you have been courting. The last time this happened, the throne was stolen by the younger brother."

"Armo sent you here to question me." Mikhail realised. "He sent you to ask if Yordan would betray me. What answer do you wish from me?"

"That we will not have to suffer a war between brothers." Her voice was sharp. "That you will marry, and quickly. That you will produce an heir with that woman and the throne will be secure."

"Yordan would live in the mountains if he could. Now that he is married, he will not take Kismet from a life she is accustomed to. But he does not want the throne. I have nothing to fear from him. I will marry when I wish and none shall question me."

She gave him the slightest of smiles. "Well said, Prince Mikhail. Now, you should ready yourself for the day. There are servants waiting outside. I must tend to other duties, but I will come for you when it is time."

Seija bowed to him as she left the room. Mikhail had only a moment of peace before the servants descended upon him. He followed blindly as they led him from his rooms and found himself in the bathhouse. His clothes were stripped and he was urged into the hot water. Mikhail wondered briefly what Neassa would think about all of this.

Soft handed servants began to scrub at him, lathering the soap against his skin. His hair was combed and trimmed. His nails were cut and polished. Everything about him was adjusted, just slightly, until he was as perfect as he could be. Soap dripped from his hair into his eyes. He pushed the servants away so he could dunk himself under the water, escaping their touch.

Everything was muted under the water. He could hear the servants talking above him, the sharpness in their tones dulled by the water. Perhaps he should have taken the tea that Seija had offered. As the time to farewell his father came closer, Mikhail's desire to hide in his chambers and refuse to come out grew stronger.

A hand touched his shoulder and Mikhail lifted his head from the water. Armo looked down at him, his wrinkled face arranged into a polite smile. The servants had gone in the short time he had been under the water. He leaned back, letting his head drop as he stared at the ceiling.

"Is there something you need, Armo?" Mikhail asked, surprising himself with how calm and even his voice sounded. "I was in the middle of bathing."

"Seija said that you would need some tea."

"I told her that I would not." He sighed deeply. "If you have come to convince me to drink it, then you may very well succeed."

"I would not try to sway your original decision. I just thought it was quite strange for you to request it, when you are even hesitant to drink the sleep tea." Armo offered a towel to Mikhail.

Pulling himself out of the water, Mikhail dried himself, discarding the towel once it became damp. Clothes were held out to him. Mikhail paused, looking Armo up and down. Why was the wise one here? Seija had said he had duties elsewhere. He pulled on the dyed black pants and began to tie them closed.

"Armo, what do you want?"

The older man spread his hands in a non-threatening gesture. "I want for nothing, Prince Mikhail. Just the safe continuance of this kingdom."

He wanted to trust the man. This was the man who had healed his injuries as a child, the same man that had fought for years to keep his mother alive. But Mikhail was no longer a child. The wise ones had their own motives, he knew that now that he was older. His hand ran through his hair, pushing it back from his face.

"Seija cornered me and asked me some questions." Mikhail explained. "I suggest you speak with her about the proper way to address a king. For I will be king."

Armo gave a low bow. "Of course, Prince Mikhail. I shall tell the servants to return and finish your preparations. It will not be long."

Mikhail watched the man until he was gone. Their motivations were unclear. But if they intended to drive him and his brother apart, they would fail. He pressed his hands to his eyes, sighing heavily. As if this day were not hard enough. If he could ignore them and leave them to their own devices without having to worry, he would.

"My lord?"

"Continue." Mikhail replied, dropping his hands. The servants helped him into the rest of his clothing, their touches light and fleeting. It was as if they were afraid. Once he was dressed, a nervous young woman had to paint the signs of mourning onto his face. Her hand trembled, the brush hovering before his eyes.

"If you cannot put the paint on my face, then find someone who can." Mikhail growled.

Tears sprung into her eyes and she dropped the

brush into the shallow bowl of paint and ran from the room. He did not follow her path to the door, staring straight ahead. Someone else stepped in front of him, but Mikhail could not focus.

His hands were tight balls on his thighs, hidden by the sleeves of his mourning robe. Mikhail hated himself for what he had said, words and actions learned from his father. But to apologise would be to show weakness. If only he had been patient. Or given her a kind word to soothe her nervousness. What would Neassa think of him?

The brush felt cold against his cheeks as the new servant applied the paints. He held himself still, though he wanted to push them all away. The paints took a long time to be applied. At least it felt like an eternity. Why must he sit through this tradition that meant nothing?

"Are you done?" Mikhail growled.

"Yes, my lord." The woman murmured.

A door opened behind him and Mikhail turned to see Seija walking through the door, clothed in mourning robes much like Mikhail's. No paints adorned her face, but her hair was pulled back tightly from her face. She bowed to him as she approached. "It is time." Seija announced.

He followed Seija through the halls, only vaguely aware of the crowd that gathered at his back. All clothed in black robes, joining him to farewell the king. He stepped into the throne room, his eyes averted from the litter that lay before the dias. The crowd filtered into the room as he climbed the stairs to stand next to the throne.

Mikhail looked down, regretting his decision to look at the corpse of his father. He lay on the litter, dressed in simple white cloth. The man's face was grey and the skin of his cheeks hung loose. Bile burned up his throat and Mikhail clamped his mouth shut. He would not be sick in front of the nobles. He would not shame his father like that.

Yordan moved to the front of the crowd, his mourning paints already streaked with tears. Kismet was by his side, watching Mikhail with her dark eyes. She had followed their traditions and donned the robes and paint. Mikhail was grateful for that. He took a deep breath, his eyes lifting to the ceiling for a moment, to centre himself.

"We gather to farewell the king." Mikhail spoke, his voice rolled across the gathered crowd, silencing the soft whispers. "King Yasen, of House Nemes, lies before us. He has left this life and gone to join his wife, Lilyana, who passed before him."

As one, the crowd lifted their hoods and covered their faces. Guards stepped forward and lifted the litter that the king was laid upon. Mikhail looked down on his father's face once more before he was carried from the throne room. Grief rooted him in place, unable to follow the guards' slow steps.

"Brother." Yordan called to him.

It felt as though Mikhail was fighting against the strength of a mountain as he stepped forward. His limbs felt as heavy as stone, threatening to spill him across the floor if he stumbled. Their eyes were on him, following him as he stepped down from the dias. Yordan touched his shoulder, but even the slight weight of his brother's hand nearly sent him to his knees.

His father was gone. He could feel the weight of responsibility crashing down on his shoulders. It was going to break him. How could he rule a kingdom so soon after his father's death? He would ruin everything. Every careful plan that his father had made would go to waste. Why had the man never shared anything with him?

"Mikhail?" Kismet's voice was soft next to him. He became aware that he had not taken a step in several moments. The crowd around him was waiting. Mikhail looked down at the threshold. A step more and he would be out in the sunlight. Just one more step and he would be out of the castle. He could follow his father and send the king off with the respect he deserved.

"If you wish to take the throne, Mikhail, you must follow him." Yordan murmured on his other side. "I do not wish to take the crown from you, but I wi-" Mikhail forced himself forward, the steps he took down the castle stairs were the hardest he had ever taken. But he would not allow Yordan to shoulder the responsibility of the crown. His brother was not suited to the task and he would not betray his father's wish by allowing Kismet to take the throne.

The sun was hot as Mikhail followed the procession from the castle grounds and up the well worn path to the cliffs. A crowd had gathered at the castles gates to follow the old king. It was slow, the men carrying the king's litter now moving at the respectful slow march that every king had been carried from the world. He could feel the sweat dripping down his back under the black robe. With the hood drawn up to cover his face, he was just another mourner in the crowd. No one special, but for the robed guards only a few paces away. Mikhail wished this were over, anything to return to his chambers and sink into his bed.

"I happened to notice a new scar on your ribs, Prince Mikhail." Armo murmured.

The man appeared at his side now that they were free of the castle and were free to spread and mingle as they made their way. A chill ran down Mikhail's spine. What reason did Armo have to ask that question now? While he was taking his father to the cliffs. Hot tears stung his eyes and he resisted the urge to wipe them away.

"I did not treat you." Armo continued. "Was this something you went to Seija for?"

For the first time, Mikhail wished he had his father's unfeeling personality. He never tolerated the wise ones and their meddling. Their questions had been rude and intrusive. If he could banish them from his castle, he would. But they were needed, as healers and teachers.

"Leave me, Armo." Mikhail muttered. "You are disrespecting me, and disrespecting my father by talking during the procession."

"Forgive me, P-" Armo began.

"No."

The man silenced himself instantly. Mikhail felt Armo leave his side, but was aware of the weight of the wise one's stare on his back. He just wanted to finish the march in peace and say his goodbyes to his father. Then he would be left alone until he decided he had mourned enough.

A warm hand slipped into his and Mikhail nearly ripped his hand from the touch. A voice stopped him, instantly soothing the stress and worries that were weighing on him.

"I am here." Neassa whispered. "Do not look at me,

or I will be noticed. I am sorry I was not there last night."

"I am just glad you are here now." Mikhail murmured, squeezing Neassa's hand gently.

CHAPTER NINE

Mikhail stepped forward from the crowd. Armo gave
him a gentle look and a lit torch was pressed into his
hands. He gripped it tightly, as if it would ground him
to this world. Yordan was beside him, a torch in his
trembling hands. He could feel the warmth of the
flame on his cheek as he took his position at his
father's head. Yordan stood by his feet. If they had
siblings, they would line up in order of age, each with
their own torch. But their family line had never been
blessed with many children.

Armo was talking, addressing the crowd that had
gathered to farewell the king. Mikhail focused on the
man's voice. He was speaking of Yasen's life, of his
accomplishments, of the life he had with his wife and
the children they had. Mikhail made eye contact with
Yordan, the younger man crying silently. Tears stung
his own eyes and he had to blink them away. No
weakness.

His gaze shifted from his father, looking out to the crowd. Neassa still stood where he had left her, clothed in the same mourning robes as himself. But she had lifted her head so he could see her face. She had painted the signs of mourning onto her cheeks, three long thin lines that started at the bottom of her eyes. The lines were streaked with tears, as all mourners' faces would be.

He finally allowed the tears to fall, their heat rolling down his cheeks to gather at his chin. Mikhail and his brother had not been allowed to cry when his mother passed, and these tears were as much for her as they were for his father. The torch wobbled in his grasp, Mikhail struggling to keep his shoulders squared and strong.

"Crown Prince Mikhail, Prince Yordan, please, release your father from his chain to this mortal realm." Armo gestured to them.

Taking a shaky breath, Mikhail dipped the torch down. It touched lightly on his father's shoulder, on the cloth that covered him. He could see Yordan doing the same, his torch touching at the king's legs. They circled the pyre, dipping their torches to the king's body in places until they had fully circled the king. By now the flames had spread across their father, his flesh crackling.

Mikhail and Yordan backed away, relinquishing their torches to the people who stepped forward to take them. He stepped back to his place, standing close to Neassa. Tears dripped from his chin, unable to stop their flow now that he had allowed them to begin. Neassa's hand gently took his, rubbing her thumb over the back of his hand.

"We farewell King Yasen, of House Nemes. And we

greet the reign of his sons." Armo's words closed the ceremony.

Mikhail could feel the crowd behind him moving from their places and Neassa's hand slipped from his. He grasped at the empty air but could not look for her as the crowd approached to share their condolences with him and his brother. Armo bowed before him, a low bow for a wise one. The old man wanted something, Mikhail was sure of it.

"Speak, Armo." Mikhail murmured.

"How long will you be staying?" Armo asked.

He stared at the crackling flame that was consuming his father. "Until it is done."

The wise one bowed to him again. "I shall arrange the guards. Will you be wanting privacy?"

"I can arrange them myself, Armo." Mikhail answered tiredly. "Go back to the castle with Yordan and take care of him."

He turned to the men that hovered around him and pointed to a guard. "You, leave your sword. I know you have it hidden under the robes."

The weapon was produced and Mikhail waved his hand to dismiss them. They hesitated, obviously unwilling to leave him alone so soon after the death of their king. Mikhail nearly yelled at the guards, his desire to be alone so strong. No harm would come to him, no harm had ever come to him, surely they could see that.

"We will guard the path to the cliffs." One of the guards spoke. "We will not be far if you need us, your majesty."

Mikhail nodded, accepting the guard's offer. Anything to be alone. He could not look for Neassa, but he was sure she was there. Armo tried to linger, but one of the guards took the man's arm, guiding him away from Mikhail. He looked hard at the man's face, burning it into his memory. That man would be rewarded.

He turned back to his still burning father. Smoke billowed above the pyre then was dashed away by the wind. Yordan had gone with Kismet back to the castle. His brother would be taken care of. Kismet was strong and had no emotional attachment to their father. She would be strong for her husband. Mikhail sat down, shedding his robe. Without the heavy black material he was much cooler.

"I am here." Neassa whispered, appearing at his side. She had shed her robe as well, standing before him in her simple cotton dress. He reached out and pulled her down into his lap. Her arms wrapped around his shoulders and pulled his face to her chest, fingers gently stroking through his hair. Mikhail sobbed against her, smearing the mourning paints over her clothing. They sat together for some time, Neassa simply holding him close.

"I am sorry." Mikhail murmured, pulling back from her.

Neassa smiled, rubbing away some of the tears on his cheek with her thumb. "Do not be. It is better for you to cry now than later alone."

He touched her cheek lightly, wiping away the paints that stained her cheeks. "You are beautiful."

Her eyes turned away from him, colour rising on her face. She watched the pyre that had burnt low while they had sat together. There was a sadness in her expression that hurt Mikhail.

"He is really gone."

"Yes."

"I am sorry." Neassa whispered. "It is hard to lose a parent."

Mikhail realised how little he knew about Neassa's family. "You have lost yours?"

"One of my mothers."

"One of?" He asked. "How do you have more than one?"

Neassa laughed shortly, ducking her head in embarassment. "My father had many wives, just as my brother does. We consider all of the wives to be one of our mothers. It is just how the selkie families work. I lost the mother that birthed me. But I had many others to take on the role. It is still hard."

Mikhail pulled her close. "Of course it is. What of your father?"

"He is still alive. He travels a lot. Visits the other selkie clans. I have... quite a lot of siblings. He may only have thirteen wives, but he has spread his seed far and wide." Neassa sighed.

"I see."

Neassa jumped to her feet, Mikhail missing the warmth as soon as she had moved. She did not look at him, moving closer to the pyre and watching the small flames that still burned there. Mikhail wrapped his arms around her from behind, his chin resting on her shoulder. This time she did not move away. Her hands laid over his arms, squeezing gently.

"Will you come tonight?" Mikhail asked.

"I do not know. Niamh has been angry with me for leaving so often." Neassa shrugged. "I think grandmother is sending her to another clan. There is a boy that has come of age. Niamh would be happy with a selkie husband, she trusts humans too little and will be lonely without me."

"Without you?"

Neassa shifted slightly in his hold but did not answer his question. He wanted to ask again, to get the answer she was holding from him. But he would not be able to stop his heart from breaking if she said she was leaving. Mikhail pressed a kiss to her cheek and was rewarded with her lips curving into a smile.

"Why did you make the guards leave this?" Neassa gestured to the sword.

"So that I had something to protect myself with." Mikhail sighed. "But I am safe here."

He watched Neassa pick up the sword and unsheath it, running her fingers along the flat of the blade. She shrugged to herself then held it out. Mikhail took it and sheathed it again.

"I've never used a sword." She admitted.

Mikhail glanced down at the blade in his hands. "I am decent with the sword. However it is not likely that anyone will reach me to put me in danger. I did enjoy fighting with my fists."

Neassa perked up at his words. "How do you do that?"

"No, that is too dangerous. I am not showing you how to fight." Mikhail said quickly.

"So you would prefer that I have no way to defend myself?" She asked.

He sighed. "That is no-"

Before he could finish his sentence, Neassa had moved, her shoulder drove into his chest, sending him stumbling backwards. Her foot lashed out and tripped him. Mikhail landed heavily on his back and, before he had the chance to respond, Neassa was sitting atop him, pinning him to the grass with a bright smile on her face.

"What was that?" He asked, giving her a slight smile.
"A little... demonstration." She laughed then bent
down and pressed a kiss to his lips. "I am not a
delicate maiden like those around you. I have lived."
Mikhail sat up, cupping a cheek gently. "I have never
thought of you as delicate."
"Then why do you insist on keeping me away from
you." She asked suddenly.
Pain thudded in his heart. "Neassa, you do not
understand."
Her hands captured his and held it to her chest. He
could feel her heartbeat under his palm. Strong and
steady. Mikhail dropped his head to her shoulder.
Wrapping his arms around her waist, he held her
tightly. They sat like that quietly, Neassa's hands
combing through his hair again.
"Explain it to me." She murmured. "What is making
you so afraid?"
"My mother was a commoner." Mikhail mumbled
against her. "She was so weak and frail. But Father
loved her. There are only two of us because Mother
was never strong enough to carry children. They
waited so long for Yordan and I to be born. I do not
want to lose you the same way Father lost Mother. He
was so lost when she died. He became so angry."
"I am not your mother, Mikhail." Neassa murmured,
her fingers in his hair again. "I am not going to get
sick, I am not going to die."
He shook his head. "It is a risk that I cannot bear."
"So you will remain alone because you are scared that
whoever you marry will get sick and die young?"
"I must produce an heir. I must marry before I can
be crowned as king." Mikhail admitted softly.
Neassa's warmth disappeared suddenly and Mikhail

looked up to see her standing above him. Pain was painted across her face. He wished to take back his words, anything to erase the hurt he had caused her.

"So you will marry another woman." Neassa murmured. "And what will I be?"

He dropped his head. "I will not take you from the sea, Neassa. That is your home. I will not watch your health fail. I would run away before I did that to you. But I cannot leave the throne to Yordan, he is not strong enough for it."

Mikhail lifted his head. He was alone. The space where Neassa had been standing was empty, the grass already springing back into place. Casting his gaze around, Mikhail scrambled to his feet. There was no sign of her on the cliffs. He turned, looking down the path. Had she gone past the guards?

"Neassa!" Mikhail called. "Neassa, where are you?"

His only answer was the rustling of the grass in the wind. He ran, following the path down the cliffs. The guards turned as he approached, their weapons drawing from their belts. Mikhail slowed, skidding a little on the rough path. Their faces were filled with worry, staring back up the path at him.

"Did a woman come past?" He asked, eyes darting to their faces, hoping that one of them was Neassa in disguise.

"No." One of the guards answered. "You were left alone. How did a woman get to you?"

"It does not matter!" Mikhail snapped. "Did anyone come past or not?"

"No one did, Prince Mikhail."

Fear jumped to Mikhail's throat. Where had she gone? He turned to look back up the path. She had not been there. This was the only way down from the cliffs. Once more he had hurt her, torn her heart from her chest. Why had he told her of his plans? Why had he not just lied? He should have been more clear that he did not want those things. That he did only want her.

"Prince Mikhail?"

He rounded on the guard. Pale green eyes met his calmly. Mikhail sighed, his anger dying as quickly as it had started. They did not deserve his anger. It was not their actions that had caused this. He would not become his father.

"It does not matter. She is gone now. I am returning to the castle." Mikhail muttered.

His chest felt hollow as he walked. The guards fell into step around him. He did not look up from his feet until he stepped back into the castle, Yordan's hand falling to his shoulder. It roused him, and reminded him of how he must look.

"What happened, Mikhail?"

"I was foolish." He murmured. "Where is Kismet?"

"She is with Seija." Yordan muttered, not meeting his eyes. "I was going to come and get you from the cliffs. It has been hours."

Mikhail shrugged off his brother's hand. "I am going to bathe. Go back to your wife."

"Mikhail!" Yordan exclaimed. "What happened up there?"

"It is none of your concern!" Mikhail roared, pushing his brother back. "It does not matter, because what is done cannot be undone. Leave me be, brother, or I will throw you and your wife out of this castle. Do not question me again!"

Shock flashed across Yordan's face, the younger man shrinking back from him. Mikhail stammered, trying to force an apology from his lips. Yordan turned and strode away, his brother's hands balled into tight fists. He was acting just like his father. The guards had been saved from his anger, but he had attacked his brother instead. His shoulders slumped and he shuffled through the castle to the bathhouse.

CHAPTER TEN

It had been a month since Mikhail had last seen
Neassa. He had waited for her to come to him in the
night, wanting to apologise, to beg her to forgive him.
He had never wanted to hurt her. And yet, he was
doing just that.

He glanced down at the young woman that hung off
his arm. She twittered at him in her high pitched
voice while he walked through the gardens with her.
If he was totally honest, he was not listening to a
single word she said. Her name escaped him at the
moment, and if he asked her for it, she would be
offended.

Mikhail had sent his guard, Anton, to search for
Neassa at the dock. The guard who had led Armo
away the day of his father's funeral. He trusted the
man and his simple honesty. But he had come back
several times with no new information. Even the
knowledge of a house of selkies along the docks did

not help in his search.

Swinging his current companion around, Mikhail began guiding her back to the castle entrance. She was the latest of young women that the nobles were throwing at him, attempting to force him into making a choice. He would need to marry soon or his crown would go to Yordan. If Kismet fell pregnant with his brother's child, Yordan would ascend. The bloodline would continue with their children. He would not make his brother suffer like that.

The woman continued to prattle on, her words washing over him. The sooner he left her at the castle, the better. He would claim some time alone and go back to the cliffs. Anton, as the new head of his guards, could accompany him. And perhaps he could ask Yordan to join also.

"Are you listening to me?" The woman asked, breaking into his thoughts.

Mikhail looked down at her. She was beautiful in a way, but her voice irritated him, and she was constantly touching her hair, flicking it over her shoulder. There would be no chance she could sit still and placid in the way that queens were required during their many public appearances.

"Prince Mikhail." A voice called out to him, a woman's voice.

He paused, turning to see another young woman coming up behind them. Her name was... His mind faltered before latching onto the memory of her introduction. Anka. Mikhail felt his current companion's fingers dig into his arm as he bowed to the new join. Jealousy would never have a place in a queen's traits. Gently, he pried her hand from him.

"Thank you for your company today." Mikhail

smiled, giving her the slightest of bows.

He could see the outrage burning in her eyes and the murderous look she shot at Anka. Her body dropped into a curtsey and she fled, nearly running from the scene. Mikhail sighed softly, glad that he was finally free of her twittering voice. A hand lifted to run through his hair, watching after the young woman he had just cut loose.

"Is she going to give you trouble for interrupting?" He asked.

Anka laughed. "I doubt it. She has been courting my brother for several months before you decided to look for a wife. I am sure she will go back to him."

Mikhail glanced away when Anka mentioned looking for a wife. It was an act. A way to stall the wise ones and the rest of the court while he waited for Neassa to return. He was beginning to lose hope. Even with his guards, it was unheard of for a king to visit the harbour unless it was for a ceremonial launching of a navy vessel.

"Is there something wrong?" Anka asked.

"Not at all. Why did you call out to me?"

She shifted slightly, not quite meeting his eyes. "I saw the look of distraction on your face. You seemed quite miserable and I was hoping to gain some favour with you for rescuing you from her."

Of course, Mikhail should have known. It was another ploy to make herself seem like a better choice. Anything to win the crown for herself and her family. His enjoyment of her company turned sour and Mikhail nodded.

"I must leave you here. There is some business that I must discuss with my brother." He bowed slightly. Confusion flittered across the woman's face and he turned away, walking briskly to the castle entrance. His first companion was standing in the shadows of the doors and she stepped out to talk to him, her face still set in irritation. He did not even pause or glance her way, brushing past the hand that reached out to him.

Vultures, the lot of them, all circling, waiting for the slightest sign of weakness. They wanted to watch him fall, to stumble along his path and lose his strength. All of them were false and two-faced. He would not bow to their will, he would not take a wife that he did not want. If Neassa did not want him, then he would take no one else.

"Prince Mikhail, wait!" Anka called to him.

He did not stop, continuing on his path through the castle. A hand grabbed his arm and made him stumble. No one dared touch him. He turned, staring down into Anka's defiant face. She did not step back or avert her eyes like he expected.

"Since you seem to think that everything is about you, I will tell you something. I am the only daughter in my family. They think it is a great honour to marry someone as respected and powerful as you." She sighed, finally dropping her eyes from his face. "I do not. I do not want to be forced into a marriage that I have not chosen. I have no interest in being queen, but if I did not try, for my family, then I am dishonouring them. I shall not bother you again today."

Her dress swished as she turned and stalked away, her steps light and quick despite the anger that Mikhail could see in her frame. He watched her go, disappointed in himself for the way he had acted. Of course not everyone would wish for the crown. It was a difficult job and took a strong person to rule.

"My lord, do you want her punished for touching you?" Anton stepped out from around a corner.

Mikhail waved his hand. "Leave her be. She did not do it out of malice. Do you know where Yordan is?"

The man bowed. "He is with Princess Kismet in their rooms. He has asked that they not be disturbed."

"He has asked that for the last week." Mikhail growled. "He is a prince and he has duties to attend to."

Mikhail strode through the halls, silently fuming about his brother's disappearance. Yordan had been distant since their father's day of farewell, and now he had locked himself in his room with Kismet. It would no longer be tolerated. He would not shoulder the burden of an entire kingdom alone. His brother had to learn that his emotions were not a reason to lock himself away from his responsibilities.

The door to his brother's rooms was closed and, when Mikhail tried the handle, he realised it was locked. Pounding his fist on the door, Mikhail waited for his brother to answer. There was a voice from the other side. Yordan's voice, asking for them to leave.

"Open the door, Yordan." Mikhail shouted through the heavy wood.

Silence met his request, time passing slowly until Mikhail heard the sounds of the door opening.

Yordan peered through a small gap, looking pale and strained. His eyes darted, finding the figure of Anton standing behind him. The door opened further.

"Your man cannot come in." Yordan muttered.

Mikhail scowled. "Why not?"

"I can only tell you if you come inside." Yordan murmured, glancing up and down the hallway again.

"Only you, brother."

Mikhail nodded slightly to Anton then stepped into the room. The guard took his position beside the door, his eyes locked with Mikhail's until the door closed. A sense of dread fell over Mikhail, now that he was alone in the room. His brother would never hurt him, would he?

His hand crept to the dagger at his belt. He had to strain to see into his brother's rooms. Inside was dim, the curtains drawn across the windows to hide the sunlight. There was no sound from further in, like Mikhail expected. Where was Kismet? Yordan touched his shoulder and pressed a finger to his lips. The gesture drew a frown to Mikhail's face but he followed his brother silently. He released his grip on his dagger.

Kismet was curled up in their bed, the blankets covering her. She was asleep, her face smoothed of any lines and worries. She looked much younger than she had before, and Mikhail realised he was not entirely sure how old she was.

They crept past the bed and stepped into a second room. There was a small table and Mikhail sat down as Yordan closed the door carefully. The younger man let out a soft sigh and dropped into a seat, his hands covering his face.

"What is happening?" Mikhail asked, his voice soft.

"Kismet is pregnant."

Mikhail leaned back in his seat, staring up at the ceiling. Yordan's words swirled around his head. Kismet was pregnant. His brother had an heir, unborn, but still tangible. He had heard no rumours around the castle, but he had never been one to listen to the mindless chatter. There was a hollow feeling in his chest.

"Mikhail." Yordan whispered. "I have not told anyone. I do not want the crown. But I do not know how much longer we can keep this a secret. You must marry."

His eyes lowered to his brother's face. "Neassa is gone. I have not seen her in so long."

"Then pick one of the girls you have been courting. I do not want the crown, and Kismet has agreed to keep her pregnancy a secret until you marry. But it will not stay like that forever. She is sick." Yordan sighed. "Did Mother have this much difficulty with her pregnancies? I am afraid. She is trying to appear strong, but she is getting weaker."

"I do not know." Mikhail murmured. "I know nothing."

A voice called for Yordan from the other room. Mikhail watched his brother slip through the door to comfort Kismet. The room's walls closed in on him, suffocating him. He stumbled up from his seat, knocking the chair to the floor.

Mikhail could not take it and strode from the room, pushing his way past Yordan. Kismet's voice called to him, sounding weak, but he could not stop. He needed air. The door was pulled open and slammed behind him, Anton standing at attention beside the door.

"Find Anka." He snapped. "Bring her to the gardens."

Anton nodded and their paths continued together for a short while before the guard split off. Sunlight filled Mikhail's vision and his steps slowed. He knew now that, even if he wanted Neassa by his side, he could not wait. The crown was his responsibility, and

Yordan did not want it, that much was clear now. Shame washed over him. Had their mother not always said that they had to protect each other? His hand strayed to the scar on his arm. Did he trust his brother so little that he believed a stranger would sway Yordan against him? No, Mikhail realised, he had learnt this paranoia and distrust from their father. He had let a broken man lead him down a path to failure. Mikhail would follow no longer.

He paced, walking back and forth in the gardens. Past the flowers that his mother had asked to be planted. Past the bench where his mother and father had sat together while he played as a child. Past the tree that he had climbed with Yordan to escape their teachers. Memories of how close they had been, and still were.

"Prince Mikhail."

He turned. Anton stood nearby with Anka, the young woman looking worried. The guard had a hand on her back, stopping her from running away. Mikhail waved the man off and he bowed. Anka jumped as the guard removed his hand and stepped back.

Moving forward, Mikhail grabbed Anka's hand. "I need you to be my queen."

Anka pulled her hand from his. "Did you not listen earlier when I said I did not want this? Have you gone mad?"

"Yes." Mikhail answered. "No. I do not want this either."

"Then why are you asking me?" Anka hissed.

"Because I do not plan to actually marry you."

Anka paused at that, eyeing his curiously. "Explain."

Mikhail led her to the nearby bench and sat her down beside him. Her fingers were laced loosely in her lap. She was a beautiful woman with hazel eyes and honey brown hair pulled back from her face. If he had not met Neassa, she would surely be the woman he would have chosen to marry. She raised an eyebrow at him, still waiting for his explanation.

"There is a woman I wish to marry. But I cannot reach her." Mikhail started. "My only choice would be to announce that I am marrying another. I am sure she will come."

"And if she does not?" Anka asked.

He looked up to the sky, watching a single cloud drift across the expanse of blue. "Then you would be queen. I ask you because, if she does not come, I respect you, I enjoy your company. You are the best choice."

"Why is there such a hurry?" She asked suddenly. Mikhail hesitated.

"If I am to help you, and potentially become your queen, I expect no secrets between us."

"Princess Kismet is pregnant." Mikhail murmured. Anka went pale, her hand lifting to her lips. They stayed like that for a long moment until she stood, straightening her dress. He stood with her quickly, watching her face. Her fingers laced together, sitting demurely against her waist.

"I see. I accept your proposal, Prince Mikhail. I shall inform my parents, and our binding should be organised within the week." Anka spoke clearly, her chin lifted high. "Thank you for confiding in me. It would have been hard for you."

She curtsied deeply then turned and began to walk away, her back straight and head held high. The perfect posture for a future queen. Mikhail watched her until she disappeared into the castle and he was left alone once again with Anton.

"I hope I have not made a mistake." Mikhail murmured. "I hope Neassa will come."

Anton did not answer. Mikhail chuckled softly at his predicament and sunk onto the bench again. The wind blew through the garden and rustled the bushes around him. It was a pleasant place to sit. His only wish was that he could have brought Neassa here, to sit with her as his father had with his mother.

"Have you ever been in love, Anton?" Mikhail asked. The guard chuckled softly. "I have three children. I will say yes."

"Three!" He exclaimed. "You are married."

"To a beautiful woman. She was very proud when you asked me to be the head of your guards." Anton did not relax his posture, but his voice softened. "I do not get to see her as often. I was working up the courage to ask if I could move her and my children into the castle."

"I would be cruel if I did not agree." Mikhail murmured. "Of course you can, Anton. I am sorry that I did not ask earlier about your life."

Anton glanced over at him curiously. "You are the king, Prince Mikhail, even if you do not yet have the crown. Why should my life be of any interest to you?"

"As my mother once said, a king is nothing but a servant to his people. He must do what is right for them, even if it is not what is right for him."

"Like marrying someone he does not know?" Anton questioned cautiously.

Mikhail slumped, his elbows resting on his knees. "Exactly like that, Anton. Exactly like that."

CHAPTER ELEVEN

He could hear the nobles on the other side of the door, murmuring to each other. So quickly, Mikhail had made his choice, they were saying. And so soon they were being wed. They knew something was wrong. She is pregnant, the prince was sampling women that were not his to touch.

Anger pulsed through him at those words. He had never done anything untoward with any of the young women he had courted. There had always been a chaperone. He wanted to punish them for talking that way of Anka, but that would only give truth to their rumours, in their eyes.

"My lord." Anton bowed beside him. "Lady Anka will be along soon. Her mother was crying and Lady Anka wanted to be sure she was alright."

"That is fine." Mikhail muttered, looking down the hall. "It will give Neassa more time."

There was a soft noise from Anton and Mikhail

glimpsed a look of uncertainty on the man's face. He did not believe that Neassa was coming. Mikhail tugged at the robes he wore, trying to make them sit comfortably. He knew Neassa would come, even if Anton and Anka thought otherwise. She would come and he would beg her forgiveness in front of everyone.

"Has she come?" Anka asked.

Anton answered when Mikhail did not. "No, Lady Anka."

"There is no more time." Anka whispered. "The doors will open soon. I am sorry, Mikhail. I know you hoped she would come."

He looked down at the beautifully painted woman. Her eyes swam with tears. Tears for both of them. Mikhail had not wanted to trap Anka into a life she did not want. He bowed low to her, hearing the gasp of surprise.

"Please forgive me."

The doors before them opened. They took up each other's hands and slowly moved towards the altar, their eyes trained on the figure of Yordan standing at the altar. He would be the one to wed them, in this hall with the eyes of all the nobles watching.

Anka lagged, her steps slowing the closer they got to the altar. Mikhail squeezed her hand lightly, to remind her that she was not alone. She did not return the gesture. He slowed to match her pace. Her family were watching, their faces glowing with pride. It seemed they had no idea that Anka did not want this.

"Anka." He whispered.

There was no response and Mikhail fell silent. They finally arrived at the altar, kneeling before Yordan, their heads bowed. Water dripped onto the stones before Anka and Mikhail looked over to see that she was openly weeping, her mask broken before anything had even begun. He turned his gaze to the floor, willing himself to be blind to her pain or he would begin crying also.

Yordan cleared his throat, readying himself to begin his speech. His voice stuttered and broke, the words faltering on his lips. Mikhail lifted his head to see his brother staring at the other end of the hall. He turned, following his brother's gaze.

Someone had thrown open the doors to the hall, and was standing in the doorway. Mikhail stood, his heart beating rapidly in his chest. They walked down the aisle, chin high. Mikhail did not know what to do. His eyes jumped between Anka and the person who had interrupted.

"Mikhail."

There was a gasp as the young woman addressed the crown prince without his title. She did not bow, she made no show of deference. She spoke his name and waited. He did not know how to respond. Mikhail met Neassa's eyes, shame running through him.

"Neassa." He whispered.

"By the laws of my people and yours, I claimed you as my husband. We are bound together by a magic that cannot be broken." Neassa's voice was cold and strong. "Why are you knelt at the altar of your people, to wed that woman?"

"Neassa, I-" Mikhail started, but was stopped by Neassa's hand.

"I claimed you to be my husband. And you have disrespected me and my people."

"No, I-"

"There is nothing you can say that will make me

forgive you, Mikhail." Neassa announced, her voice rising so all could hear her words. "You had the chance to fulfil the bond and you cast me aside. You are cruel, just like your father."

Mikhail stumbled down the aisle as Anka pushed him forward gently. Neassa was turning away, already leaving. He could not let her go. His hand caught her arm. Pain blossomed in his chest as she drove her fist into him, sending him stumbling back.

She stood over him, her eyes which were usually filled with love, empty and emotionless. Neassa turned back to the door, leaving him where he was.

He would not let her go this time.

"Mikhail, do not let her leave!" Anka shrieked.

Neassa paused in her steps. Mikhail returned to the altar, helping Anka to her feet. She smiled up at him, hope in her eyes. He smiled.

"You are a very beautiful woman, and I would be lucky to have you for my queen. But I am in love with another. I cannot turn my back on her. Not now that I can have her in my arms again." Mikhail bowed to her. "Forgive me, for causing you pain."

"I forgive you." Anka whispered. "Thank you."

Mikhail left Anka by the altar, racing back to Neassa's side, grasping her hand and lifting it to his lips. She watched him, her eyes still cold. He touched her hair softly, wrapping the curls around his finger, then drew her close to press his lips to hers.

It took a moment for her to soften, to melt into his embrace and press her body to his. It was when her arms looped around his neck that Mikhail knew that she was his. And he would never leave her again.

Whispers spread from them, until the hall was filled with the buzzing of confusion.

He pulled back, touching Neassa's cheeks and brushing away the tears he found there. "Neassa, I choose you to be my queen. I choose to have you by my side for the rest of my life. I choose to love you and grow old with you. Will you choose me?"

"Mikhail, I choose you. I choose you, not to be my king, but to be my husband. I choose to stay by your side." Neassa replied softly.

He guided Neassa to the altar. She went slowly, their eyes locked together. He did not care what was going on around him, only that she was by his side once more. They knelt together, Yordan's voice rising over the crowd. Mikhail squeezed Neassa's hand gently, and she squeezed back.

"Speak the vows." Yordan encouraged.

"I hold your hand in mine, a guide for where you step." Mikhail started, his entire world narrowed to Neassa's eyes. "My heart belongs to you, a treasure no one else will take. My love for you will never fade, until the day I am released from this world. Your eyes are my stars, guiding me home. Your smile is my sun, giving light to my life. Your hands are my fire, warming me when it is cold. I love you, Neassa, and I take you as my wife."

Neassa's eyes were shining with unshed tears, a smile lingering on her lips as he spoke to her. Mikhail could not have spoken the words with such meaning to Anka. He was happy, happy that Neassa had returned, happy that she had taken his hand and come to the altar.

"I place my hand in yours, guided by your strength. Your heart is mine, precious beyond all gold and jewels." A few tears escaped Neassa's eyes as she spoke. "Until the day we are both released, our love is eternal. I am your stars, and I will guide you home. I am your sun, and I will give you light. I am your fire, and I will warm you when it is cold. I love you, Mikhail, and I take you as my husband."

Silk touched their hands as Yordan bound them together, a physical representation of their bond. Neassa could not hold back her tears, the droplets running down her cheeks.

There was such joy in her eyes that Mikhail could not help himself. He leaned forward and kissed her softly.

"King Mikhail and Queen Neassa." Yordan announced, holding his arms wide.

They turned, Mikhail guiding her carefully. As they looked over the crowd together, they bowed, the nobles shifting in place, soft murmurs spreading through the crowd about the events that had happened. Mikhail did not care. He had Neassa by his side, and he was never going to let her go again.

"Come, my queen." He murmured to her. "We must go and greet the people."

Neassa hesitated. "Will they accept me?"

Anka stepped forward, her face washed clean of her paints. "They will love you." She said, answering for Mikhail. "I wish you great happiness. And many children."

Mikhail smiled softly. "I am sorry, Anka. For all I did to you."

Her smile was broad. "You were forgiven the moment you released me. Thank you, Mikhail."

There was a hand on his back and Mikhail found himself pushed through the crowd, Yordan at his back. The younger man was laughing, trying to get them through the nobles that tried to stop, each wanting a word with the new king.

"King Mikhail!" Kismet threaded her way through the crowd, looking tired. "I hope you have chosen well." She looped her arm into Yordan's and they followed as Mikhail led Neassa through the castle. Cheers rung through the halls, spilling from the windows. The commoners began their cheers as the sound reached them.

"Wait, Mikhail." Neassa stopped him before they stepped into the sun.

Kismet and Yordan stopped with them, curious as to what was happening. Neassa fiddled with her clothing, scuffing a bare foot across the ground. Mikhail waited, patient. They would have no secrets, but he would not push her if she was scared.

"Mikhail... I am pregnant."

Neassa's eyes flew to Mikhail's face as he squeaked, throwing his arm around her and lifting her from the floor to spin her. She squealed, shocked by the display and clung to him tightly as well she could with one free hand. He lowered her back to the floor and drew her lips in for a long kiss.

"Did you hear that, Kismet?" Yordan murmured. "Mikhail has an heir."

"I heard, Yordan." Kismet answered dryly. "Does this mean we can tell others about mine?"

Mikhail drew Neassa out into the sun before she could ask Kismet what she meant. His hand held hers tightly, easing her forward one step at a time towards the castle gates. The commoners saw them, roars of excitement going through them as they saw that, once again, the royal family had married below their station.

Neassa pressed herself into Mikhail's side, hiding

against him. A fond smile was on his lips and he pressed a soft kiss to the top of her head. Deep brown eyes looked up at him, happiness shining in them. They were together. And they would be together forever. Mikhail led her back from the castle gates, leaving behind the sound of cheering.

The gardens rustled around them as Mikhail sat on the bench, drawing Neassa close. Carefully, his hand touched her stomach, amazed that his seed had taken root. He was going to have a child.

"You have made me so happy." Mikhail murmured. "I will never hurt you again."

A smile lit up Neassa's face and she leaned forward to kiss him again. "No, you will not. I will never leave you, Mikhail. This is all I wanted. I love you."

"I love you, too."

AUTHOR'S NOTE

Thank you for reading *Mikhail*. I poured a lot of love into this story and I hope you enjoyed it. Please be sure to leave a review! Your feedback is always welcome and your word-of-mouth keeps my books circulating. Be sure to keep an eye out for more of my books, there are many more tales on their way!